A Grave Every Mile

A Pioneer Western Adventure

David Fitz-Gerald

David Fitz-Gerald

Cover design by White Rabbit Arts

Edited by Kolton Fitz-Gerald and Lindsay Fitzgerald

Welcome

Welcome aboard!

Ghosts Along the Oregon Trail was written as if it were a single volume rather than a series of five novels. It has been divided into five books which split the Oregon Trail into segments, or legs, of the journey. Readers will enjoy this series most when read in order, beginning with *A Grave Every Mile*.

The following map is presented to help you navigate the migration from our jumping off point in Independence, Missouri all the way to our destination along the Clackamas River. On the map, we'll follow from the bottom right corner to the top left.

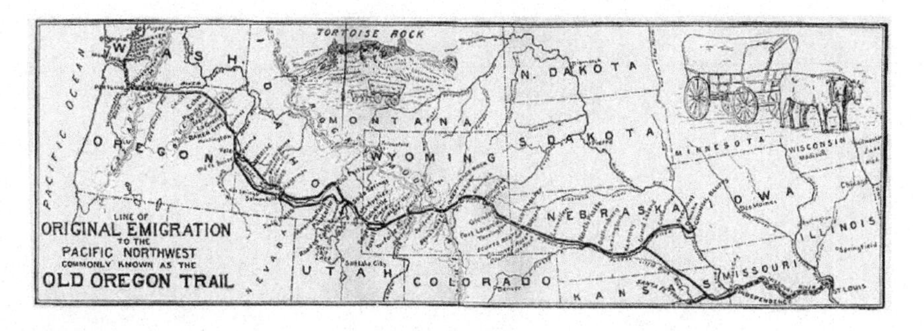

The Ghosts Along the Oregon Trail series features a large cast of characters. A list is presented at the end of the book to help you keep track of them. You may prefer to reference the roster at:

https://www.itsoag.com/gatot-cast

Contents

Saturday, April 13

I hate it when men fight. After a man throws his first punch, he doesn't remember why he's fighting. Where's the marshal? A town the size of Independence *must* have a lawman.

A crowd gathers in the rutty street as two men face each other, circling, waiting for an opportunity to swing. The blond combatant hollers in a high-pitched voice, "Take that back, Bobby."

The dark-haired man, evidently Bobby, shouts, "No, I won't. You can't make me."

The other man shouts, "You can't talk about my wife like that. I'll rip your head off."

"She may be your wife, Wayne, but she's also my sister. I'll say what I want."

Wayne lands a glancing blow on Bobby's cheek. As the punched man's face turns, I realize these aren't men. They're practically boys.

The crowd cheers, encouraging them on. I've heard enough. If nobody is going to stop them, I will. My youngest daughter whines as I slide her from my hip, and wails when her feet reach the boardwalk in front of the dry goods store. My twelve-year-old daughter's eyes reflect trepidation and I reassure her. "Don't worry, Rose, honey. Hold Dahlia Jane's hand.

Stay right here until I return, and please don't wander off, for Heaven's sake." I glance about to see where my husband and the boys are, but they're nowhere in sight. Not that Larkin would intervene. He would just shake his head and frown.

Two steps from the walkway, in front of the mercantile, my boots meet the muddy, uneven street. Even over the heads of observers, now three deep, I peg the fighters. At times like these, being a woman who is taller than most men is an advantage. As I push people aside, the two men growl at each other. Their arms lock as the evenly matched scrappers transition from fisticuffs to grappling. A trickle of blood dribbles from the corner of Bobby's mouth, and Wayne has a crimson eyebrow.

A tidy-looking young woman catches my attention. First, she addresses the dark-haired man, evidently her husband. "Stop it, Bobby." Then she reprimands her brother. "Knock it off, Wayne. You are creating a scene. Somebody will get hurt." She glances up at me, her brow furrowed. It seems like a plea for help. I should know better than to interfere in the business of strangers. How many times have I been warned not to get involved? I can never help myself in such situations.

I step toward the snarling bruisers, grab each man by the back of his shirt, and separate them. The scrawny hooligans are surprisingly easy to lift. Maybe they seem so light because of all the years I spent chopping wood. The brown-haired man squirms more than his opponent, who implores, "What are you doing, lady? Have you gone mad?"

"My name ain't *Lady*. It's Dorcas, or Mrs. Moon, if you must." Their dangling legs barely reach the ground. I clutch wads of fabric in my fists and their feet dance urgently beneath them, trying to find purchase within the muck. I feel like a schoolmarm interrupting a playground scuffle, but these are not children. I gaze into the dark eyes of one boy, then the bright eyes of the other. "What's gotten into you? I'm sure you know better than to behave like this. What would your mothers think to see you now? You should be ashamed of yourselves."

The people around us shuffle out of the way, and I'm surprised by an oncoming carriage. It's too late to duck to the side of the street. A team of shiny black horses swiftly conveys a magnificent rig through a gloppy puddle a few feet from the boys and me, drenching my pink checked dress in pungent mud.

I'm distracted by the sound of a man speaking in a strange accent to another gathered crowd across the street. I release my grip on the quarrelsome youngsters, dropping them into the sticky wet dirt, and trudge toward the mob.

Even above the clattering sounds of emigrants departing the civilized world, his musical tone catches my ear and turns my head. The *most* breathtakingly handsome man I have ever seen towers heads above the people surrounding him. I can't hear what he's saying, but his commanding voice draws me through the crowd, and his intriguing lilt dances in my ears. His dark eyebrows raise, and the corners of his mouth tip upward as if he is amused to see a woman listening to him. There aren't any ladies other than me in attendance, though I'm not much of a lady, truth be told.

The orator stands atop a stump at the edge of Maple Street facing Public Square. His light-brown cheeks remind me of the surface of a freshly baked cake, just pulled from the cookstove. The flapping wings of a giant butterfly tickle the insides of my belly. I remind myself that I am *not* a maiden, as I often do when I see an attractive man.

He continues pitching to the crowd with his eyes locked onto mine as if he's speaking only to me. "You could set out on your own. That is a good way to feed the vultures and wolves, yes? You could choose another outfit to guide you across the wild prairies and barren deserts. Why should you join us? Nobody knows the west better than we do. We are born of these lands, and we have made the trip many times before."

Finally, the charismatic speaker looks away and introduces three comrades. First, he presents the wagon master, Joseph Roulette, who reminds me of the lumberjacks from my hometown. The man on the stump says, "You may call him *Boss Wheel*." Next, two solemn scouts are introduced. "They will hunt game and look out for your safety along the way."

My husband, Larkin, arrives beside me. Half the time I cannot find him, yet he always seems to materialize when I'm indulging impossible romantic thoughts. "Come along," he says.

Holding a finger to my lips, I say, "First, let's have a listen." I turn slightly away from Larkin, hoping that he will listen closer to them if he's not trying to nudge me away.

A committee of three men from Indiana is introduced. Their leader, Reverend Mortimer Meadows, explains that they have formed a company to govern the affairs of the traveling village as it wends its way toward the distant Pacific Ocean. Despite his standing with God, he tells us to refer to him as *Captain* Meadows. It is hard to concentrate on what the man says. When the flat-faced preacher speaks, his long, hooked nose twitches while he talks. Not just the knob on the end; Captain Meadows' entire nose wiggles about as he pontificates. I imagine I could ride a toboggan down his nose and become airborne when the sled reaches the tip.

I'm glad when the younger man begins speaking again. His words flow in a gentle cascade and the resonant tone dances in my ear. There is a magnetic quality to the way he speaks. A tantalizing blend of passion and grace wraps around my senses like a hot cup of tea, thick with honey, beside the fire on a winter evening, warming me from the inside out. Even basic words and simple sentences are enchanting.

As he introduces himself, I say his name repeatedly, committing it to memory. Agapito Huerta Delgado, the assistant wagon master, is from Santa Fe, and he invites us to call him Pito, if we prefer, but I think I like the sound of his full, given name better. He completes his sales pitch by saying, "Step right up, sign the contract, and join our company. *Bienvenidos.* Welcome, *mis amigos.*"

With his speech finished, Agapito nimbly jumps from his stump and stands before us. Even standing on the ground, he is among the taller men assembled. He's not quite as tall as I am, but nearly as tall. His friendly brown eyes and boyish good looks are even more arresting close-up. He extends his hand toward my husband and says, "I am Agapito."

I turn my head slightly, wondering what my husband is thinking. Hopefully, he feels compelled to sign a contract at once. He says, "It is a pleasure to meet you. My name is Larkin Moon, and this is my wife, Dorcas."

Agapito speaks like he is singing a song. "It is a delight to meet you, Dorcas." I have never heard my name pronounced like that. The r rolls off his tongue, and the s hangs unspoken at the end. He takes my hand in his and bows ever so slightly. For a moment, I feel like Isabella, the Queen of Spain. "Are you emigrating to Oregon? Will you be joining our company today?"

Larkin tells Agapito that we will discuss it with our friends who are traveling with us. As Larkin asks Agapito a couple of questions, I watch Bobby and Wayne sign a contract and shake hands with Captain Meadows. The jovial young men seem to have forgotten their quarrel. They triumphantly slap each other on the back, now seemingly the best of friends.

As my attention returns to the men beside me, Agapito hands Larkin a piece of paper. "Here are the things you need in your wagon for traveling to Oregon."

Larkin tells Agapito that we already have everything we need. We have spoken with family and friends about the necessary provisions. Agapito asks whether we have talked to anyone who has made the trip before, and Larkin sheepishly shakes his head. Agapito implores, "Please take the paper. Bring what it says. Only what it says, yes?"

My husband raises an eyebrow. I know what he's thinking. The list surely does not include the iron safe that takes up so much room in our wagon. Since before we were married, almost fifteen years ago, Larkin has dreamed of being a banker, and the brand new safe that we purchased on our way to Independence is just what he needs to get started in the business when we reach Oregon. Having never left the town we were born in, I readily agreed to help Larkin chase his dream. No matter how much people warn us, I can't help thinking of the journey as a grand adventure.

I suddenly remember having left the girls outside of the shop and I'm itching to get back to them. I tell Larkin, "I think it would be wise to follow guides from the country we are traveling through."

Larkin complains about the price. "I expect we can find cheaper guides, Dorcas."

We have known each other since we were children. As a young girl, I was sweet on Larkin's best friend, a handsome, half-Indian boy named Noah, who still makes my heart skip a beat when I think of him, even now. Larkin and I often bickered as youngsters, even arguing about trivial matters, and that hasn't subsided through the years. But our safety is not an inconsequential matter. "Larkin, our lives could depend on who leads us. We should not be miserly when it comes to this decision." He *hates* it when I call him a miser.

I watch as Larkin stands before me, our feet sinking slowly into the muddy street. He twists the pointy ends of his mustache, which could mean that he is irritated, distracted, or doing figures in his head. I say, "Let me take the list while you think about the wagon train. Please talk about it with our friends." My eyes dart about, looking for the boys who are nowhere to be seen. With a shake of my head, I pluck the list from Larkin's hand and return to Rose and Dahlia Jane.

The girls are sitting on the wooden walkway, leaning against the building, and they grumble at me. Rose glowers and asks, "What took you so long? Did you forget about us again?" Dahlia Jane whines for me to pick her up.

"Your father and I had some business to tend to, but never mind about that. Let's see if there is anything we need inside." Diverting grumbling children from whatever complaints they have is a strength of mine.

The shopkeeper greets us pleasantly as we walk into his store, then sneers as if invisible fingers pinch his nose when he notices the mud on my dress. I scan the list as we make our way slowly through the crowded store. It is reassuring to see that we have many items on Agapito's list.

As a baker, I have lots of flour, sugar, and saleratus to ensure that my cakes rise. I don't have enough dried fruit. Dehydrated apples are better than no apples at all when making pie, and dried pumpkin is good too.

The shopkeeper talks me into buying lemon syrup, which will improve the murky water we'll find along the way. He suggests two bottles, so I purchase three to guarantee we'll have enough, and so that I can flavor scones, one of my specialties. He also recommends peppermint extract, and I can't resist. I buy a dozen blank journals and ten lead pencils. I hope to have enough paper to keep the children busy along a 2,000-mile trip. I may even keep a log myself. Agapito's list has the word trinkets on it. I ask the shopkeeper, "Mister Ray, can you tell me why I need this?"

"Yes, ma'am." Mr. Ray looks down his nose as if telling me something he thinks everyone should know. "The Indians along the way expect you to provide them with gifts, like tolls, in exchange for passage through their lands. Would you like me to make some suggestions?"

The idea of buying presents for Indians fills me with excitement and I nod my head. I'm unsure whether it is the thought of meeting them or trying to find things they might like. I overlook the impertinence of the judgmental shopkeeper. Mister Ray suggests beads, tobacco, hand mirrors, and shirts. I buy more than he recommends. Then he asks, "Do you have any India Rubber, Mrs. Moon?" As I purchase thick, slippery rain gear for everyone, I hope that Larkin will not ask me how much it costs. I hope to distract him by telling him to make room in the wagon for a couple of sacks of cornmeal. According to the list, my supply is insufficient.

I must admit having lost track of time. As I leave the store with my first armload of provisions, Larkin, our two sons, and friends from home are in a celebratory mood. The contracts have been signed, and we have officially joined a company of wagons, as I had hoped we would.

Larkin says, "Dorcas, why don't you help everyone with their shopping?" I tuck my purchases away, tell the boys to stay with the wagon, and head back toward the mercantile to help our friends as one of the storekeeper's assistants delivers the cornmeal to the back of our rig. Because of a sign in the window, our black friends, the Banyons, may not enter, so I purchase apple vinegar, dried beans, and coffee on their behalf. Mr. Ray, who has just finished sweeping dust and chunks of mud from the floor, sneers as I step back into his establishment. He doesn't seem glad that I've brought him more business.

It is late afternoon by the time everyone has completed and stowed their purchases. We're about to climb into our wagons when we notice townspeople scurrying from the streets and boardwalks, taking cover indoors.

A couple of tough-looking men appear on the street, facing each other, hands hovering at their sides, guns in their holsters. This isn't like the young men throwing fists a few hours earlier. The air feels thick with tension. I swallow hard and realize that one of the two men is about to die. We hasten around the corner onto Liberty Street just as the sound of gunfire explodes in the air.

I was the last to make it safely around the bend and the first to peek back around the corner.

One man stands, leaning backward, arms stretched and laughing menacingly. The other has dropped where he stood, limbs akimbo, in a heap on the muddy street.

People who had ducked for cover moments earlier return to get a closer look. A thin man in a brown vest steps into the street. Two men follow closely behind him, amble toward the dead body, lift the man from the road, and carry him away like doing so is an everyday occurrence. This town is nothing like the ones back home. Though I don't know them, I'm curious about the quarrel that compelled their duel.

Larkin steps forward, Dahlia Jane in his arms, and says, "Let's go now. If we survive Independence, the rest of the trail should be easy."

A shiver halts me briefly, as Larkin's prediction of smooth sailing ahead disappears into the air. We climb into the wagon and I turn, notice that

Rose is missing, glancing about, hoping to spot her. She's halfway to the place where the gunfighter fell in the mud. I shout for her to come back, but she doesn't seem to hear me. I leap from the wagon. More mud splatters my dress, but I run to find her.

When I catch up to Rose, she's rounding the corner, seemingly following the men who carried the dead body. Where are they now?

I'm right beside Rose, yet she still doesn't happen to hear me. I reach for her shoulders, shake her gently, and repeat her name. She glances at me quickly, then looks back up the street, directly at a building with a sign that reads, "Undertaker." The foul air reeks of rotten eggs, moldy bread, and hot manure. I guess that's what decaying human bodies smell like. As the carried corpse disappears within the structure, Rose turns back toward our wagon without a word.

When I catch up to her again, I ask, "Rose, honey. Is there something the matter? Do you want to talk about it?"

She shrugs. "No. Why, Mama?"

I'm confused. It's like nothing has happened, or she has already forgotten about following the cadaver. I shake my head and wonder where her mind goes sometimes.

Usually, we walk alongside the wagon but this evening, we ride as passengers while Larkin walks beside our team of six oxen, in three teams of two, led by Hardtack, our gentle giant, and Scrapple, his partner. Larkin never rides in the wagon, because he says it makes him seasick. An hour later, we join a dozen wagons, already settled into an encampment.

Our boys, Andrew and Christopher, who are eleven and nine, tend the oxen, and Larkin pitches a tent beside the wagon. It is harder than usual to make sleeping space among our belongings with extra provisions crowding our confined footage. With limited space inside the vehicle, Larkin and the boys will sleep in a tent, while the girls and I slumber under the cover of a canvas wagon bonnet, crowded by cargo.

Last fall, we left our home, in the Adirondack Mountains of New York State, moving as swiftly as oxen can go, arriving in Missouri before the worst of winter's weather. We rented a vacant cabin with our friends for a couple of months, living together in tight quarters before striking out again, arriving in Independence early this morning. It's hard to complain about all the things we left behind when everything we own is packed into such a small space. I almost wish we'd left more things behind.

When I finish tucking the girls in, I nestle myself among sacks of provisions and inhale deeply. The rich, sweet smell of cornmeal fills my nostrils and I close my eyes. I should be thinking about rolling forward into the future with my family, but all I can think about is the dashing assistant wagon master, Agapito Huerta Delgado. What kind of a name is that? Where we're from, nobody has such musical sounding names.

Even if I were unmarried, it would be foolish to think about such a handsome man. My mother always told me that the good-looking ones are nothing but trouble. I tell myself that I am happily married, but sometimes, I am not a good listener.

Sunday, April 14

I COULD MAKE PANCAKES in my sleep, even outdoors. I stretch as I build a fire and yawn while I stir the batter, thinking about the grand adventure to come. Many women in camp complain about leaving established homes for a hardscrabble migration, but I look forward to making this trip.

Andrew and his younger brother, Christopher, enjoy the excitement. Ever since Rose turned twelve, she has grown increasingly quiet. She rarely confides in me anymore. Dahlia Jane says things like, "Aren't you sad that we don't have a home anymore?" I assure her that we do have a home, and we take it with us everywhere we go, like turtles. Yesterday, Dahlia Jane said, "I don't want to be a turtle." Perhaps Rose and Dahlia Jane will relish the journey once it gets started in earnest.

Andrew, my serious boy, is the first to awaken and join me beside the fire. "Good morning, Mama," he chirps. He has a journal beneath his arm and a pencil in his hand. I ask him if he's hungry and if he's working on a project.

"Yes, Mama, I'm on assignment. I've decided to start a newspaper. Every day, I'll print the news and post it each evening. I could nail it onto the side of our wagon. What do you think?"

I turn to face Andrew, surprised at his suggestion, though he's always coming up with something unexpected. "That sounds like a splendid idea. What will you call the newspaper?"

Andrew mentions a few ideas. He says, "My favorite choice is: *The Rolling Home Times*." Before he can tell me the other choices that he likes less, the rest of the family joins us. Andrew looks disappointed. Hopefully, we'll get a few minutes alone together later in the day.

Christopher, my adventurous boy, rubs his eyes and grumbles. "Why didn't you wake me up?" He looks around and frowns. "Aren't we leaving today? I can't wait to get started." Christopher is a lot like me, eager for adventure.

Andrew says, "It's Sunday. We leave tomorrow. I told you that already, Christopher."

As I pour another pancake into sizzling grease in the cast iron skillet, a couple of wagons roll up, sending dust into the air. I reach for a tin plate and place it over the rim of the bowl to keep dirt from my batter, wishing I could also cover the cake in the pan. Larkin says we will eat ten pounds of dirt in six months along the trail. I'm beginning to believe him.

Dahlia Jane nibbles on a pancake, which she holds in her hand and eats without syrup. Between bites, she says, "I want a kitten."

I look at her and say, "Me too." Then I think about all the animals that we are taking with us. Truthfully, I am glad we don't have more critters to worry about.

We have eight strong, rust-colored Devon oxen, a broody red hen with a handful of chicks, a crotchety milking goat named Ridge, and a black and white Andalusian stallion named Blizzard. I could look endlessly upon the spectacular whorls of color on his coat. He's not just a treasured friend but a work of art. An eccentric, wealthy old man from our hometown gave me the spirited horse because my baking pleased him. He said that the

Andalusian is exceptionally hardy in regions with scarce grass and water, like the great desert ahead of us. Blizzard is genial, especially for a stallion, unless somebody else tries to ride him. It infuriates Larkin that he can't ride my horse. It makes me love Blizzard all the more, knowing he will not allow anyone but me to mount him.

After breakfast, Larkin asks the children to tend the animals as Agapito appears beside our campfire. Rose leads the bleating goat to water as I offer Agapito a cup of coffee. He declines and says, "I must gather the emigrants. We shall meet at the demonstration grounds on the hill in half an hour." He points to a slight roll of the prairie, which I wouldn't bother to call a hill. He tips the brim of his hat, looks into my eyes long enough to see into my soul, and saunters off to the next wagon.

I follow Agapito to the Banyon's wagon to see if Jennie needs help with her morning chores. It pleases me that Agapito doesn't treat the Banyons differently from white travelers.

Jennie is slight, frail, and seven months pregnant. She gratefully accepts my help feeding her children, Bess and Joe, who are six and three. Her husband has a kind smile. His name is Charlie, though everyone calls him Cobb.

I've never seen a couple of people more desperately in love. When Jennie looks into Cobb's eyes, her head tilts to the side, and she just stares at him until somebody says something. Usually, it makes me happy to see, but sometimes I feel envious. If only everyone loved their mate as much as Jennie and Cobb do, the world would be a better place.

Cobb dreams of having an apple orchard and has brought a dozen potted seedlings along with him. Jennie talks of sitting and sewing all day in his orchard when they get to Oregon. Cobb has a small herd of yearling Devon cattle, in addition to his team of oxen, given to him by the abolitionist, John Brown. They come from a community of free men and freed slaves near our hometown, called Timbuktoo, which John Brown founded to teach subsistence farming.

I offer to escort Jennie to the hillside, and she looks to Cobb before taking my arm. Cobb says, "I'll be right behind you with the young'uns."

On the crowded bump of a hill, Agapito stands with his retinue holding a trumpet. He lifts the instrument slowly to his lips. I glance about, and nobody pays attention to him until he begins to blow.

After a couple of notes, quiet descends upon the crowd, and Agapito speaks. "*Buenos días*, and good morning *amigos*. Tomorrow when you hear Reveille, arise at once so you may start your pilgrimage, yes?" I wonder why they roust emigrants with the song that the military uses to wake up soldiers.

At Captain Meadow's request, we will not travel on Sundays. The trumpet will sound at 3 am, and we shall depart at four. Agapito introduces Boss Wheel, who steps forward, places his hands beside his mouth to amplify his voice, and croaks, "I am a man of few words, much experience, and many rules. If you have complaints against one another, take them to Captain Meadows. Otherwise, I'm ramrodding this expedition."

Boss Wheel recites a long list of rules. I've always had trouble following regulations, and I'm sure there are more than a few of Boss Wheel's pronouncements that I failed to hear. He tells us to direct all questions to Agapito, "That's what he is here for." He barks, "You are to leave my scouts and me alone."

I'm astonished by Boss Wheel's manners. If I were him, I would offer words of encouragement to paying customers. Instead, he says, "I cannot guarantee that you will make it safely to Oregon before winter. Many of you will perish before we arrive. You will experience hardships and great sorrow on the trail ahead. This is the cold hard truth and your last chance to turn around and go home." He concludes his remarks with a grunt.

Agapito waits a few moments as if letting Boss Wheel's words hang in the air before he calls out names. He assigns each wagon a number and tells us that we shall travel in the same order, every day. Agapito says, "Wagon number one will lead on the first day, then move to the rear on the second day. On the second day, wagon number two shall take the lead, and so on, until every wagon has taken a turn at the front and back." As he calls out the wagon assignments, I can feel my eyes widen in surprise, and my heart beats faster when he says that his wagon is number fifteen and ours is sixteen. I know I shouldn't think about a man who is not my husband in the way I do, and try to blink my thoughts away as if exiling them to the wind.

Whereas Boss Wheel lists rules, Agapito provides valuable information about the trail. Each night we'll form a circle with the wagons. The next day's lead wagon will point its tongue to the north, so we will always know which direction is which, even when the clouds obliterate the sun. Though, I'm sure, several men have compasses. Men and older boys will be assigned night watch in rotating shifts. Everyone must also take turns driving the extra cattle and horses that will travel a short distance from the wagons, slightly behind. Regardless of the weather, we must look after our stock. Younger boys will take turns driving Agapito's wagon.

Agapito says, "We invite you to attend demonstrations today. At ten, I will teach women and children to load and shoot rifles and handguns. If attacked, our survival may require that we defend ourselves. We will show you how to maintain and operate your wagons at two o'clock. That will increase your odds of surviving the two-thousand-mile trip, yes?"

I haven't shot a gun since before I married Larkin. I recall having a good eye and wonder if I'll remember how. There's a flutter of anticipation in my belly that my corset can't contain. All I can think about is shooting practice while scrubbing our clothes against the ridges of a washboard in a bucket. As I launder my pink checkered dress, I am glad my apron is brown, as muddy water splashes from the pail. I hang the dress I wore in Independence on a peg outside the wagon, and wonder when I'll get the chance to wash our clothes again. Perhaps not until next Sunday.

Finally, I've removed the mud from everyone's clothing. I ask Larkin what time it is. Instead of answering, he says, "How many times must you ask me that?" He grumbles, pulls his watch from his vest pocket, peers through his round spectacles, and says, "Twenty minutes until ten. I don't know why you need to learn about guns. As I remember, you were a better shot than most of the men in town."

I look down into his eyes and say, "That was many, many years ago, Larkin." I strap my bonnet over my hair and poke a few stray strands inside. It doesn't matter how many times a day I braid my tresses. Nothing I do seems to keep them in line. If only I had a corset for my hair.

On my way out, I turn back toward Larkin and say, "See that you have dinner ready when I return." He shakes his head from side to side and smiles. I laugh and see a glimmer of the lighthearted, joke-telling roustabout that Larkin was as a boy. It takes all the restraint I can muster not to skip away like I often did as a youth.

Jennie declines to accompany me, choosing to spend the morning sewing, instead. I'm relieved that Esther Bump says 'no' as well. I like Esther, who is also pregnant and expecting a baby even sooner than Jennie, but Esther is a fussy worrywart. I always struggle to keep from getting aggravated when her face gets all twisted up.

Addie Bull is one of my dearest friends from home, and I'm glad that she and her family have come along with us, but she is afraid of almost everything. I don't know why Esther aggravates me more than Addie does, but when Addie starts voicing her fears, I look for somewhere to hide. Perhaps it is *because* of her worries that Addie decides to join me today.

Agapito approaches with an amused expression. I wonder if he enjoys teaching women how to shoot. "We begin with the rifle," he says. "This is a Hawken, muzzle loading flintlock rifle. Here we have a powder horn. This is a ramrod." His eyes connect with mine for a moment before he looks away. He continues slowly in short sentences. "Measure a charge of black gunpowder. Pour it down the barrel. Set a patch on the top of the muzzle. Place a lead ball on top of the patch." With a fast punch of the short-starter, he sends the bullet partway down the barrel. I watch his slender fingers as he thrusts the ramrod down the barrel, punching the ball down against the powder. He explains what could happen if we fail to push it in far enough. Then his gaze scans the crowd of gathered women. Out loud, he asks himself, "Who should go first?" Then he answers as if he already had decided. "Mrs. Appleyard, would you please fire the first shot?"

The doctor's wife steps forward like she has just won a prize at the county fair. Agapito stands behind her, and it looks like his chest touches her shoulders as he positions her to fire the rifle, then he steps away. He tells her to look down the barrel, line up the sites, and squeeze the trigger when she's ready. As Charlotte fires, she jerks the gun upward, sending the bullet into the sky. She laughs and says, "I believe I have shot the sun."

Agapito invites Charlotte's daughter, Violet, to try next. When she shoots, she screams. The bullet kicks up dirt, short of the target. She rubs her shoulder and says, "It's like being kicked by a mule."

When I look back at Agapito, he's grinning at me. "Would you like to meet the burro, Mrs. Moon?"

I resist the urge to tell him I have some firearms experience as my feet step forward. The empty tin can that once held slippery peach slices shines in the bright prairie sun. My heart thunders in my chest as Agapito stands behind me. A slightly sweet and citrus smell, like lemonade, accompanies his presence, and I wonder whether it is due to soap or cologne. Often, men don't smell good, but this one does. I tell myself to concentrate on firing the gun. His hand grips my forearm, and he tells me to look down the barrel at the target. Then he lets go and steps away.

I know I've hit the target as soon as I squeeze the trigger. I am confident, knowing the outcome in that fraction of a second before the bullet kicks the can into the wind. I turn to Agapito, hand him the rifle, and say, "You are an outstanding teacher, Agapito."

"Are you toying with me, Mrs. Moon? You have fired a rifle before, no?"

I feel my cheeks redden. "Not since I was a girl. I thought that I had forgotten how."

"Let us see if you remember how to load it." He watches as I pour the black powder down the barrel. Then he asks Addie to step forward and take a turn. She jerks the rifle to the right as she fires. It is good that the crowd of women stands safely behind the shooters.

After everyone takes a turn, Agapito teaches us to fire and clean a *revolver*. When I hit the target again, he says, "I shall call you Dead Aim Dorcas. Are you sure you are a housewife? You are a dangerous outlaw woman, no?"

I can't help but giggle. "I can throw axes, and I'm good with a rope too."

Agapito holsters his gun and raises an inquisitive eyebrow. "How does a woman learn such things?"

I shrug. "I come from a small town full of lumberjacks at the edge of the wild woods, and as a girl, my mother had a tough time keeping me at home. She said I was a gamine, wilder than my brother. Mother often claimed that it was good we lived on the frontier because a city or town wouldn't do for a girl like me. Perhaps, she was right. I never did take to sewing, and I don't like to clean. Fortunately, I make up for it with my cooking." As usual, by the time I realize that I'm talking too much, it is too late. I back up into the group of women, hoping to disappear among them. But the crowd is breaking up anyhow.

Agapito asks if I'd like to try again at a greater distance as if he hopes to prevent my escape. Addie says that we should be getting back.

I wave her off. "Why don't you go on without me. I'd like to practice a bit more."

She mutters that I'm already the best shot of all the women as she turns away and walks back toward the encampment.

After a couple of successes, I finally miss a shot the third time Agapito moves the can back. Then he cleans the guns, slowly and methodically. He glances up at me periodically as we talk.

After a pause, my curiosity gets the better of me. "Pardon me if it is impolite to ask. Are you a Mexican?" He confirms his ancestral origins. Then I reply, "There aren't any Mexicans where I'm from, but I always thought they would be shorter than you are."

The man laughs at me and says he always thought *women* were shorter than me. He adds, "I never met a six-foot-tall woman until now."

I snap, "I'm not six feet tall." I've always been defensive about my height. I realize my tongue is overly sharp, and endeavor to soften my tone. "I'm a full eighth of an inch shorter than that."

He laughs and says, "Oh, I see." Perhaps my drooping posture slices off a few more inches as I look at the ground. I'm self-conscious when people mention my height, and the truth is, I've never met a taller woman. What's more, most men are shorter than me. It is impossible to ignore such a fact.

Mercifully, Agapito changes the subject. "Why are you and your family going to Oregon, Dead Aim Dorcas?"

I kick an innocent clump of prairie grass, and answer, "Larkin has always dreamed of being a banker but settled for running a hotel, shop, and post office until the owner sold his business. I worked in the restaurant, making breakfasts, and baking for the guests. Larkin wanted to go to California, but I worried that being a banker in a mining town would be too dangerous, so we compromised on Oregon. I told him that farmers need banks too, especially in the land of milk and honey."

"I see." His dark brown eyes look intensely at me, and he asks, "What is *your* dream, Dorcas?" Then he looks back at his work.

I think for a moment and say, "To get my family safely to Oregon."

"Then what?"

"To help Larkin become a banker."

"I see. No, what is your dream, Dorcas? Not Larkin's dream."

I sputter, not knowing what to say. "Should a woman have a dream?"

There is a distant look in Agapito's eyes as he begins to answer me. "Everyone has aspirations." He focuses his gaze on me, and continues, "Let me ask you another question, no? Think back to when you were a girl. What made you happiest?"

As I think about Agapito's question, I sway my hips, making my skirts swirl about my ankles. Many years have passed since I was a young girl. "I used to love to ride horses, every chance I got. I'd take the small road out of town and go as fast as I could, my hair blowing in the wind behind me and the horse's mane flowing in front of me." As I finish, I realize that I'm thinking of Noah again. After all of these years, why do I still think of him and the life we could have had?

When I look back at Agapito, he's staring at me with his big brown eyes. "There is more, yes?"

"Oh, I suppose so," I say, looking away. "What does it matter anyway?"

"You are thinking of love, yes? I can tell by the look in your eyes."

"Oh, it's nothing."

"I think it is everything. When you love someone, you try to help them make their dreams come true. Just as you want to help your husband become a banker. You must love him very much. He is a lucky man, no? But hopefully, you will find your dream too. If it were not for dreams, I do not think anybody would travel the long road that lies ahead."

When I ask Agapito what his dream is, he grimaces. He looks down at the guns beside him and is quiet for a minute. Then he slowly says, "I guess I am in between dreams at the moment."

"I'm sorry, Agapito. I don't mean to pry." It is the first time I have seen him when he wasn't cheerful and friendly. What could make him so sad?

"Do not be sorry, Dorcas. I do not mind. Most of the time, I think that love is everlasting and that there is no obstacle that love cannot overcome. Other times, I am afraid that love evaporates like fog. What do you think, Dorcas? Does true love transcend time?"

"I'm afraid that I'm the wrong person to ask." As I laugh, hoping to lighten the situation, the nervousness within my manufactured giggle is apparent even to my ears.

A slight frown crosses his cheeks. A tiny dimple draws my eye to the corner of his mouth. He shrugs and says, "We can speak of it another time, but we should be getting back now, no?" He slips the gun into its holster on his right hip, carries the rifle in his left hand, and dons his pointy hat. After a glance to ensure no one has forgotten any belongings, Agapito nods toward the wagons. He says, "I feel safer knowing that we have a gunslinging gamine in our company. Someday you will have to show me how you throw an axe."

I gasp, "Oh my goodness." What have I done? This man must think I'm an absolute barbarian. An image of Joan of Arc on a white horse carrying a spear comes to mind. When uncomfortable, I'm known to carry on like an idiot. I blather, "Good heavens, Agapito. Sometimes I get carried away."

Agapito laughs heartily. His good mood seems to have returned, and I am relieved. As I walk away, I replay the conversation in my head, and can't stop wondering why he became pensive when discussing the subject of true love.

When we return to camp, Andrew greets me. His normally earnest expression shows his excitement. He points to a wooden box with a sloped top on a post in the middle of the circled wagons. Andrew chirps, "It's the newspaper, Mama." I almost have to run to keep up with him as he drags me by the hand. "You unfasten the top like this, then swing it up, see? A tack fastens the newspaper to the underside of the lid. That way, if it rains or is windy, it won't be ruined. Stillman helped me."

"Deary me, Andrew. How clever. Can I read it?"

"Sure, Mama. Anyone can. Anyone who can read, anyway. I've seen a couple of people walk over and look at it." Andrew smiles at me proudly. "Every morning, I'll take it down and set it back up each afternoon."

I tell Andrew that I'd like to save each issue of *The Rolling Home Times* as a keepsake. It will make a treasured remembrance of our journey. I finish reading Andrew's inaugural issue, introducing himself, and his passion for newspapers and journalism. He also lists the name of every family and their assigned wagon numbers, in order: Meadows, Crouse, Latham, Weaver, Carpenter, Shaw, Humphries, Sawyer, Pierce, Steele, Lett, Blocker, Reid, Appleyard, the wagon master and staff, Moon, Southmaid and Wilson, Banyon, Bump and Prindle, Bull, Bond, Horton, Gains, Grosvenor, Franklin, Knox, Grimes, Young, Franzwa, Bellows, and Nye. The lengthy list sounds more like an army than a list of travelers.

On the way back to our wagon, Andrew says he'd like to interview someone different for the newspaper every day, in addition to documenting the trip. I also want to meet everyone, and volunteer to accompany him when he introduces himself to the string of strangers. How long will it take to get to know *everybody*?

Something catches my eye when we're almost back to camp. A few wagons from our own, Bacon Bump stands on a barrel, painting something on his wagon bonnet. I don't know what possessed his mother to name him Bacon, but it's his honest to goodness name, not a nickname. His mother, Coriander, is also named after food.

Bacon is a gifted artist from our hometown, but he looks like he might fall from his perch. We detour slightly to get a closer look. By chance, I hear the shrill whistle of a steamship on the Missouri River, a couple of miles distant, as I glimpse the image of such a boat on Bacon's wagon cover. Though we came by land, many emigrants arrive at the so-called, *Jumping Off Point* by steamship. What's more, many travelers refer to their wagons as if they were floating transportation rather than land based vehicles.

One of Bacon's murals decorates the walls of our church, back home, and yet thinking of it doesn't make me homesick. I holler up to Bacon, "What a splendid picture." Bacon's wife, Esther, fusses over a campfire while her children, Robbie and Ellen, watch. I wish Esther a good afternoon and return to our wagon.

Historically, the unusual artist was remarkably uncommunicative, but has become more social since marrying Widow Prindle, last year. Even so, he does not respond to my compliment. Walking away, I hear another loud whistle. What fun it would have been to arrive in a chugging barge with a giant paddlewheel.

As I prepare dinner and bake what seems like a week's worth of biscuits, I can't help but think about Agapito and firing those guns. I jump when

Larkin steps up beside me. "Do you reckon we ought to see if we can learn anything more about prairie schooners?" I think of an illustration I saw somewhere of an armada, dozens of ships in formation on an open sea, and concede that such symbolism has merit.

I was hoping to find a way to attend the training myself, and answer, "I suppose so." The 1,300-mile trek to Independence on well-established roads is good but not adequate preparation for the two-thousand miles of wilderness ahead. I can't resist watching the assistant wagon master speak in front of a crowd, though I wouldn't want to admit it out loud. Perhaps I am infatuated, but as long as it remains my secret, what's the harm in it?

Larkin says, "We should all go to the demonstration. The children must learn to tend to the chores. The boys can grease the axles, gather wood, and carry water from now on. Rose can do the milking, washing, and sewing. We shouldn't have sheltered them from all this work last fall."

Larkin shouts to Rose, Andrew, and Christopher. I wrap the biscuits in cloth, secure them in a basket, pick up Dahlia Jane, and set her on my hip. Larkin says, "Let her walk. She's not a baby anymore. She can walk on her own."

I set the toddler back on the ground and walk toward the demonstration grounds. My family follows, several feet behind me. I'm not in the mood to bicker with Larkin today.

Monday, April 15

The sharp blast of Agapito's trumpet sends me flying from beneath the comfort of my blankets at three. It is dark, and we have one hour to feed ourselves, yoke the oxen, and prepare for our first full day on the road. My heart pounds with excitement. After saving for years, waiting for months, and making a long journey to get to our jumping-off point, I'm eager to begin.

Leaping from the wagon, I see an endless sky, littered with twinkling stars. I hasten to build a fire for coffee and pancakes.

Somehow, the rest of the family went back to sleep after Reveille. I hear muddled voices nearby, surmise they're coming from the wagon master's camp, and tiptoe a few feet through the darkness until Boss Wheel and Agapito's words are clear. I shouldn't be eavesdropping on their conversation but can't help myself. Good thing it's dark.

Boss Wheel says, "I'm worried. It is too early to start out. The grass isn't growing yet, it is the rainy season, and the river crossings will be dangerous. But, we must leave early. Captain Meadows wants a day of rest each Sunday. That means we will lose a month along the way."

Agapito sounds more optimistic. "Maybe it is for the best, no? After the crowds we saw last year, maybe it would be better to get out in front of them."

Boss Wheel grumbles. "Yes, Pito. You might be right. Hopefully, we won't have another cholera outbreak this year." I hear a heavy sigh as the former mountain man exhales. "I hate the first part of the trip. Ready or not, we have a new herd of greenhorns. Hope they're a better lot than last year's."

It seems that they have finished their conversation. Does Agapito feel the same way that Boss Wheel does? I return to our campfire and make batter as fast as possible. After dropping the first pancake into the skillet, I roust Larkin and the boys, speaking to them through the canvas tent. "Get up, sleepyheads. We must hurry. What time is it, Larkin?"

He grumbles words that a family man ought not to say in front of his children. "This lumpy prairie grass is murder on a man's back."

I remind him, "We must adapt, and we shall overcome." Larkin is particularly grouchy in the morning.

"Easy for you to say. You didn't have to sleep on the cold, hard ground."

Sometimes I can't help but poke the bear. I needle, "It's bound to get worse before it gets better."

"Is that supposed to make me feel better *today*?"

"I don't have time to bicker with you this morning unless you want me to burn your breakfast."

Larkin emerges from the tent, clutching the small of his back in his hands. Speaking to Andrew and Christopher, Larkin says, "I'll yoke the oxen. You break down the tent." He growls on his way into the darkness to retrieve our cattle.

Somehow, we've managed to feed the children, harness the stock, and stow our provisions, just in time to depart at four. As Agapito blows nine quick notes on his trumpet, I jump into the sky. I guess three sets of three blasts is the signal to begin our exodus. Andrew realizes that he has forgotten his newspaper stand, and runs to dig the post from the hub of the ring of wagons, making quick work of its retrieval.

Our three teams of oxen, led by Hardtack and Scrapple, stand ready to do their job. It takes a while before it's our turn to begin pulling, with fifteen wagons ahead of us. When the wheels of the wagon before us begin to turn, Larkin cracks the bullwhip and shouts, "Hi-yah!" He snaps the whip again, and the poor beasts lumber forward.

The broody hen squawks in her box. Straps hold the cage in place on a shelf on the wagon's exterior. Ridge, the devil-eyed goat, blats in protest as the rope that ties her to the back left corner of the wagon drags her along. I can't see Blizzard, tied to the other corner of the wagon. The children and I begin on foot, following closely behind Larkin.

I hate it when people are cruel to animals. I should hold my tongue, but I cannot. "Must you snap that whip so sharply? It's barbaric. We should thank the oxen, not whip them."

"Don't be ridiculous, Dorcas. I'm not whipping them. I'm whipping the air above them. You know that. We can't get to Oregon if the oxen don't move. Don't carry on like a child."

Of course, he's right. Somehow, dressing a deer doesn't phase me. I can snap a chicken's neck and pluck its feathers, but the idea of hurting beasts of burden saddens me. "Couldn't you just tap them lightly on the rump rather than scare the poor creatures?"

"Look, see, we're already falling behind. We need to drive the oxen faster if we want to get to Oregon before winter."

"But..."

"That's enough, Dorcas. Don't pester me anymore."

My molars tighten against each other. I know a woman shouldn't bicker, argue, or nag. Usually, Larkin doesn't complain about having a garrulous wife. Still, it rankles when he tells me not to pester him.

After walking alongside for half an hour, Dahlia Jane says she is tired. One mile down, one thousand, nine-hundred and ninety-nine miles to go. I lift the child into the wagon. Fortunately, she is content to play quietly by herself.

I walk for a while beside Blizzard. He always seems to listen and understand me when I share my troubles, worries, and complaints. His coat is sleek beneath the palm of my hand. I can never resist stroking his neck. "We'll take a ride together soon. I promise."

Dahlia Jane hasn't moved from her nest in the back of the wagon, so I return to walk with the other children. I'm surprised to find Christopher where Larkin was. Larkin is missing. I glance about and don't see him anywhere. Andrew smiles and says, "Nature calls." Rose slaps her forehead and looks at her hand to see if she squashed a bug. Christopher seems to have mastered snapping the bullwhip above the oxen, and it makes me cringe even more than when Larkin does it.

After half an hour, Larkin tells Rose it's her turn. She had been complaining about boredom and appears to have come alive as Larkin calls out her name. "Alright, Rose. Here is the whip. Hold it high and flick it hard with your wrist so that it snaps in the air above the kine."

Rose asks, "What if I accidentally hit them with it?"

Larkin answers, "Don't worry. It will not hurt them. They have thick skin and dull nerves."

I can't help but say, "Larkin, how do you know how they feel? Please don't beat our animals."

Larkin replies, "We'll try, but the children must learn how to drive them. If you can't bear to watch, may I suggest you visit our neighbors?"

"Very well, then." It doesn't make it any better knowing they whip the beasts while I'm gone, but I pluck Dahlia Jane from her burrow and wander back to the next wagon.

I walk for a few minutes alongside a pair of young men who embarked on this journey with us last year. Eighteen-year-old Stillman Southmaid was an apprentice cooper who helped build our wagons. His 20-year-old cousin, Carter Wilson, is a polite farmer who we do not know very well, despite sharing the trail with them for half a year. I inquire, "How are you men doing?"

Carter answers, "Right fine, ma'am."

"That's good, Carter. But please, call me Dorcas." I smile and hope that my words will not sound harsh. "I don't know how many times I have to tell you that."

Stillman is far more outgoing. He pipes up, "Carter can't help himself. He was born polite."

I laugh. "I wish I was born that way. Some days I feel like I shall never master having good manners. In case I forget to ask you, please stop by and visit us anytime. It looks like we're going to be neighbors all of the way to Oregon."

Stillman's chest puffs out, and his shoulders pitch back proudly. "I can't wait to get there. I've got Oregon Fever something fierce." Stillman and Carter look at each other and chuckle. I feel like I have missed the point of a joke, which happens more often than I'd like to admit. I shrug, wish them a pleasant day, and head back to the next wagon.

Jennie Banyon's eyes look dull, though her smile is bright and warm. She says that she is tired but refuses to ride in the wagon for fear that the jostling will make the baby come too soon. Though I am envious of Jennie and Cobb's love for one another, I am glad I'm not pregnant. Though Jennie is only twenty-five, she seems frail. Their children, Bess and Joe, run back and forth, tagging each other. Bess looks like her mother, except she's missing two front teeth. Joe has a constant grin and a lively sparkle in his eyes. Cobb hopes for more fertile soil to the west, and hopes for greater acceptance in Oregon. Perhaps things *will* be different in a new land. Cobb gently taps an ox on the rump with a quirt. I shake my head and wish that Cobb would teach Larkin to be more gentle with our teams. I tell Jennie I'll check on her again later, and ask her to let me know if she needs anything.

I step back to the next wagon and admire the completed steamship on the Bump family's bonnet. Esther walks stalwart beside her son, Robbie Prindle. The boy is thirteen and has slightly crossed, blue-gray eyes and large freckles. I notice that his hair matches the rust-colored Devon cattle.

Esther has a neckerchief tied across her face. She gripes, "I worry about all this dust from the trail. Sometimes I feel like I'm choking on it. I don't think it's good to breathe it in all day." Maybe she worries that it will harm her baby. There's no guessing how many women on this journey are pregnant, but it would be easy to wager that Esther's baby will be the first one born along the way. Despite Esther's fussiness, she marches across the prairie, as sturdy as an ox. When I can't listen to her complaints any longer, I promise to visit with her more later. Bacon rides in the back of the wagon. Painting seems like enough of a challenge without being pitched about in a wagon. Even when he strokes canvas with his brush on flat earth, he winds up with specks of paint in his bushy blond eyebrows. I ask what he's working on, and he tells me he is painting a portrait. Esther's daughter, Ellen, who is ten, sits inside the wagon, posing. Until Bacon married Esther, I always thought he was an awkward man. It is hard to remember Bacon doing anything besides painting a picture. Though he's currently occupied with the task of painting a subject that resides in his household, Bacon hopes to paint the landmarks on the way to Oregon.

Pious and Addie Bull ride with their children in the next wagon. They are just a couple of years older than I am. Pious is a religious man, as a man with such a name is expected to be. Addie has bright blond hair, and a warm, cheerful smile. After Jennie, she is my closest friend, though she is frightfully timid. Addie is afraid of almost everything, and even more than the rest of her fears, she is petrified of river crossings. I ask her why she decided to go to Oregon, given her trepidation, and she says that she believes it is God's will, and that she will find God's blessing in Oregon. Pious is a good match for Addie, and he seems to live to help her settle her fears, only, he's afraid of the river crossings too. Their 18-year-old son, Pious Bull Jr., is known as PBJ. Mary is seventeen, and Leander is eleven.

I have completed visiting with our friends from home, but can't resist walking back a little farther. I introduce myself to Bobby and Serena Bond. Bobby is the dark-haired, blue-shirted young man I first encountered brawling on Liberty Street in Independence, and Serena is the tidy-looking woman who appealed for help with just her eyes. Bobby doesn't look old enough to be married, but they tell me that Bobby is twenty and Serena is nineteen. I ask about the blond man in the red shirt. Bobby says that his name is Wayne Horton. I'm surprised to hear that Bobby and Wayne are best friends. I'm given to think that sometimes, the best friends are also worst enemies. Each man has married the other's sister. My head begins to ache as I try to imagine what life is like for a pair of couples, so intertwined. If nothing else, Bobby and Wayne agree that life is better having left their domineering fathers, and fathers-in-law, behind in Pennsylvania. Despite my first impression of these young boxers, they seem far more likable along the trail. After a few minutes with Bobby and Serena Bond, I introduce myself to Wayne and Drucilla Horton in the next wain.

In the distance, some eight wagons farther back, a strange looking cart rolls beside the wagon train and catches my attention. It's pulled by the largest donkey I've ever seen. I say to Dahlia Jane, "Look at that. Would you like to meet a donkey today?"

"What's a donkey?"

"It's kind of like a horse, but smaller."

We stand still and wait as the in-between wagons roll by, and greet the people who pass by until the funny cart reaches us.

I introduce myself and Dahlia Jane to a barefooted teenager. I look back and forth, between him and the unusual cart, and can't help staring at his feet. They aren't just the largest I've seen, but also the hairiest. My curiosity overwhelms me but I can't think of an appropriate question to ask. As he passes us, he turns his head, and smiles down at us. "My name is Oskar, ma'am. Oskar Franzwa. From Washington."

With a glance at his family's wagon, and a turn to follow Oskar who hasn't stopped moving forward, I introduce myself and my daughter. Then I ask about his rig, looking back at his monstrous trotters. He flips a thumb over his shoulder without looking back. "That's a machine that measures the miles as we go along. Take a good look at it, and you'll see those gears turning."

The wooden discs look like sawblades. As the rig moves along, one of the gears turns, and every so often, it moves another gear. It's hard to see how many gears there are in all. When I catch back up to Oskar, he says, "Impressive, ain't it? Don't know how it works, but you can ask Papa." He flicks his head toward the family wagon, which is unlike all the rest. A middle aged man sits on a small bench attached to the side of a wagon that looks more like a rolltop desk than a prairie schooner. Instead of the usual, useful tools attached to the side, there are curious looking gadgets tacked to the sideboards. Oskar says, "Take a closer look if you want, ma'am. Papa won't mind."

I thank the youth and step toward the wagon. First, we meet Oskar's mother, Minna, and his siblings, Alma, Bruno, and Lilly. Then, Oskar's father's seat swivels away from the desk, I can feel my eyes blink rapidly and I take a step back. With a wobble, I catch my step and prevent myself from falling backward onto the prairie as Dahlia Jane begins to laugh. It's a struggle not to follow her lead. With a cough to prevent myself from giggling, I introduce myself and shush my daughter.

The right half of the man's face is heavily bearded, and the left half is clean shaven. I've never seen anybody groom themselves in such a fashion. To avoid staring, I look down and notice that the barefooted man has enormous, hairy feet, just like his son.

The man pats his knees and leans forward. "Pleased to make your acquaintance, Mrs. Moon. I'm Fritz Franzwa." A mild German accent is detectible in his voice. Before I can ask him about it, he continues, "I am a surveyor, map maker, and inventor."

Dahlia Jane points at the side of Fritz's wagon. "What's that?"

His diamond-shaped eyes widen. "Inquisitive child."

Fritz points to a dizzying array of brass and glass gadgets, saying their names. "The anemometer measures wind speed, the barometer quantifies air pressure, the hygrometer records humidity, and several thermometers capture the temperature." Numerous rain gauges assure that Fritz will have plenty of data about precipitation. He explains the technicalities of how the odd contraptions work, in excessive detail, until Dahlia Jane interrupts him, pointing to the top of the cart. "What's that?"

"Haven't you seen a weathervane, child? The wind catches it, swings its arms, and reveals the wind's direction."

"It looks like a rooster to me."

"Yes, child. But the arrow tells where the wind comes from."

Dahlia Jane points to the west, and says, "It comes from there."

Fritz pensively taps his chin. "I guess we do not always need science to tell us which way the wind blows."

When Dahlia Jane says, "Where's the rest of your face?" I slap my mouth in embarrassment. It isn't like a child to overlook something so unusual as having a beard only on one side of the face.

With his hands on his cheeks, Fritz says, "Oh, I usually forget to mention that. Most people find it surprising. It's a protest, child. I don't believe in symmetry. It's not natural. Nothing in nature is perfectly symmetrical, but we humans always try to make things so, nevertheless. Plus, it takes away from the strangeness of having werewolf feet."

I gulp and Dahlia Jane laughs and points at the man's toes. They're so hairy, it's impossible to see the separation between them. Fritz looks into my eyes, and must read the terror in my mind. "But we're not werewolves, we just have impossibly large feet. That's all." He shrugs and doesn't look away from me as he finishes, "No need to be afraid, child."

My brother, Erastus, always used to delight in terrifying me with tales about werewolves. He would describe them in grisly detail, stalking their prey and dismembering their victims. He often recounted a story about the time that he saw a werewolf in the distance, one afternoon, stalking a bear. Now that I'm older, I'm sure he made the whole thing up, but I've been afraid of wolves as long as I can remember.

A loud clicking sound comes from the wagon wheel, providing a welcome distraction. Fritz says, "That measures the miles. There's a peg near one of the spokes. It turns a gear. Every so often, the gear twists a threaded rod. As it spirals away, it turns the gears that measure the revolutions of the wagon wheel. Three hundred and sixty rotations equal a mile. We should reach our destination after 720,000 turns of the wagon's wheels."

With a sideways glance at Oskar, I ask, "But isn't that what your son's cart measures?"

Fritz turns his head sideways, making the difference between the shaved side of his face, and the bearded half, look even more unbalanced. "I'm not content to measure things one way, Mrs. Moon. I like to be sure, you see?"

The man points to his surveying tools, strapped to the wagon, and begins to explain how they work, but Dahlia Jane yawns and rubs her eyes. I interrupt him and say we'd better be getting back to our wagon. "You'll have to tell us about that another day. It's time for Dahlia Jane's nap."

The German man chuckles, and says, "We'll make a scientist out of the child yet."

I make my way back to our wagon, place Dahlia Jane in her spot in the rear, and check on Larkin and the children. Visiting with fellow travelers has made the morning go by quickly. Everybody has had a turn driving the oxen except for me. Christopher hands me the bullwhip and giggles at the face I make at him. He can tell that it makes me uncomfortable, but is amused, nevertheless.

The oxen seem to follow the previous wagon without needing my assistance. As I walk beside them, I can see the distance widen between our oxen and the back of the wagon before us. The cattle require encouragement to keep up. Otherwise, they shall slow down until they're no longer moving. I gently tap them on their hindquarters with the end of the bullwhip and make gentle clucking noises. They flick their tails and scarcely notice my presence. I beg them to go faster, so I won't have to crack the whip.

Larkin's patience finally runs out. Snidely, he says, "Would you like to reach Oregon this year, or next?"

I have to admit that he is right. I hand Larkin the whip and ask him to show me again how to flick it so it doesn't hit them. Then, I try snapping the whip.

"You must shout at them, too. Don't whisper in their ears like you do to the horse. Yell at them like you yell at me!"

"Very well. Hi-yah! Get along, you grouchy, no good, rotten, mustache twisting, vest-wearing, sour-bottomed grumpuses." I look back at Larkin, who wrinkles his nose like he smells a skunk. Then, I crack the whip so hard I conjure sparks in the air. Their pace quickens, and they begin to catch up to Agapito's wagon. An ox bellows, and I feel a tear in the corner of my eye. At the same time, I feel powerful.

When we stop for dinner and a two-hour rest, I'm surprised that I'm not tired. I've spent long days in the kitchen and serving meals at the inn. Sometimes, I've been exhausted, having been on my feet all day. Nonstop walking, at a slow pace, seems less tiring. Perhaps it is because each foot only spends half the time on the ground.

I make a fire, fry bacon, heat coffee, and pass out biscuits. Agapito rides up to us, and from the back of his bright, golden buckskin horse, he asks how we're doing.

"No complaints," I answer, looking around at my family as they nod in agreement.

I compliment Agapito's horse, and he tells us that his mare is named Rio. "That means River." I admire the tall black socks and matching mane on the gold-colored animal. Agapito wishes us well and rides into the next camp as if he is making rounds.

Andrew tells me he needs to interview somebody as I put away our provisions. I suggest he begin with the wagon behind us and work his way through the wagons. "You could start with Stillman or Carter." Andrew says that interviews will provide material for days when nothing happens, or there are no landmarks to memorialize. Between Bacon's paintings and Andrew's newspaper, we shall never forget this journey.

I continue my turn as a teamster after dinner. Larkin walks beside me, and before long, he begins complaining about his aching back. He frowns at me when I call him an old goat, and then he complains about the dust.

I tell him that Esther is wearing a neckerchief over her mouth and nose to keep from choking. Then, Larkin complains that he feels dizzy, and his stomach aches. I tell him that he is carrying on like a spoiled child, and he mutters something unintelligible. I suggest, "Maybe you'd feel better if you whipped the oxen." I hand him the bullwhip and walk away. It's only the first day on the trail. I don't know if I can go six days, let alone six months, if I must listen to complaining all day long.

I walk behind the wagon and talk with Dahlia Jane. She tells me about a world full of people who have bodies like humans and the heads of cats. Children are so creative. A picture flickers in my mind of humans with wolf heads, and feet like Fritz Franzwa and his son, Oskar. I force the image from my mind, telling myself that they can't help it if God gave them big, hairy feet.

Our first full day of migration ends at about four in the afternoon. I watch the wagons way beyond us arc to the left, from the middle of the train. In the distance, I see the golden mare leading the first wagon as it wraps the line into a circle. As the loop closes, the lead wagon becomes the last wagon, and the second wagon points its tongue outward, to the north.

The day has remained clear and cool. While I make supper, Rose sits on the back of the wagon, writing in her journal. Dahlia Jane draws pictures in the dirt with a stick. I ask Andrew about his interview, and he tells me that he is writing about Stillman and how he was knocked unconscious when he slipped on hail while climbing a mountain last year. Christopher brings water from a small creek as Larkin unhitches the oxen from the wagon. Christopher pitches the tent for the boys while Andrew pounds his newspaper stand into the ground with a rock.

I watch Bacon Bump walk toward Andrew with a brush and his painter's palette. They exchange a few words, and Bacon grips Andrew's shoulder before Andrew runs back toward us. "Bacon's painting a sign on my post, Mama."

"Supper's ready, Andrew." I give him a tin plate with a thin slice of ham and some cornbread, and then call in the rest of the family to grab their plates. "We'll all go take a look after we eat, Andrew."

The sky begins to darken quickly. It's still only the middle of April, and the longest days of the year are a long way off. On the way to see Bacon's lettering, I ask, "What should we call this place?"

Andrew says, "You mean where I put the newspaper?"

"Yes. I think it should have a name."

"How about, 'The Hub.' What do you think of that?"

Rose says, "The newspaper already has a name. Who cares what you call the place where you put it?"

She turns away when I tell Andrew that I think The Hub is a fine name. Despite the darkening skies, other emigrants wander toward The Hub to read the second issue of *The Rolling Home Times*. The headline reminds us that we shall soon leave the protection of our country in the land beyond the States. The article explains that we'll travel through unorganized territory, much of the way, before entering the newly organized Oregon Territory, beyond. The editorial that follows Stillman's interview suggests that we *all* have Oregon Fever and are following the same trail, together, to realize our collective hopes and dreams. The newspaper's content is impressive work for a journalist of any age. To think an eleven-year-old could create such a publication.

We walk back to camp, and the children retreat to their sleeping quarters, the boys in the tent, and the girls in the wagon. I ask Larkin if he's feeling any better.

He rubs his belly, and I believe that I can see his legs wobble. I feel bad that I walked away from him earlier in the day. I tell him I hope he's doing better in the morning and step forward to kiss him good night, but he steps away and ducks into the tent.

Standing alone in the dark, I recall the conversation overheard this morning, between Boss Wheel and Agapito. Hopefully, they don't see *me* as a greenhorn, but I suppose it would be tough to argue that Larkin is anything but. I just pray that he doesn't have cholera. The mere mention of that word sends waves of dread through me. Hopefully, we'll never need to use the cholera drops I purchased from Mr. Ray, but if we must, they had better work as advertised.

Tomorrow will be a long day if Larkin doesn’t get a good night’s sleep.

Tuesday, April 16

Reveille sounds at three, and I'm grateful for the interruption. I shiver in fear, recalling a nightmare in which a pack of giant wolves rips my family to shreds while I watch, shrieking and powerless. They growl, snarl, and have oversized fangs. Their mouths are full of bloody flesh ripped from the bones of my loved ones. I shake my head, hoping to dislodge such disturbing images. I leap from my blankets like our wagon is on fire, and the dew-covered grass wets my feet as they hit the ground.

The weather is cold and damp. A fine mist falls from the sky as my fists rub my eyes, and I climb back on board the prairie schooner. I towel my feet dry before putting on my boots and don the India rubber rain gear, purchased in Independence.

My tinder catches a spark despite the rain, and I blow life into a small fire. I'm glad that I had the foresight to stow some wood in the wagon, in case of rain. I make a big pan of hot corn mush and a pot of coffee before the rain drowns my fire. Larkin is surprised when I pass out the rain gear, and he tells me that he is glad he married a smart gal. If he knew how much I spent, he might say otherwise.

I ask him how he's doing. He says that he feels much better as long as he keeps his head up and looks off where the earth meets the sky, no lower and no higher. But, it is impossible to see the horizon through the fog.

As it rains, Andrew and Christopher take down the tent, Rose milks the goat, and I help Larkin yoke the teams. It is time to roll at four, and I'm amazed at how fast an hour went by.

Standing beside our teams of oxen, I hear enormous raindrops splatter on their thick hides. Even so, when Larkin cracks the whip, they respond, just as the wagons behind us do when it is their turn.

Though we have three pairs, our muscular oxen are hard-pressed to keep our wagon rolling across the waterlogged ground. Every pound of freight they drag slows the procession and keeps us from our goal, but I wish we could let all of the children ride in the wagon.

The golden mare rides toward us. Agapito shouts above the wind. "Keep them rolling. Do not stop for anything. If we stop, we sink. We will be miserable if we have to push wagons out of the mud all day, yes?" Then, like Paul Revere, repeating his message over and over again, Agapito rides on down the line.

The oxen bellow their complaints, and Ridge bleats her satanic echoes. Larkin plods through the mud and rain for a couple of hours without fussing. By mid-morning, that changes. He starts with, "We should have gone to California instead of Oregon."

"What are you talking about, Larkin? The trail to California and Oregon is the same for at least half the trip. Besides, we agreed that mining towns aren't good places for a man with a wife and four children."

Stubbornly, he repeats an old argument. "It's a good place for a man whose fortunes depend on a safe. Oregon may be the land of milk and honey, but all the gold and money is in California. I am sure that if we had decided to go there, we would be having better luck than we are having now."

That's such an idiotic statement that I don't even bother to reply. Some people complain like it helps to pass the time. I think bellyaching just makes one more miserable. Fortunately, Andrew and Christopher are holding up well enough. When I check on the girls from the back of the wagon, Rose complains about being bored. She doesn't seem impressed when I suggest that boredom doesn't sound like a bad thing compared to the icy wind and driving rain outdoors.

We manage to keep the wagons rolling nonstop until about noon. Agapito rides down the line saying that we will not be stopping for a mid-day meal. I figure we've traveled twelve miles, and wonder how many miles we need to go before we can stop.

We go down a slight decline. Larkin snaps the whip and screams at the oxen. The wheels sink into the mud at the bottom of the little hill. Our Devons bellow and strain but are unable to dislodge the wagon. Larkin keeps pushing them, nevertheless.

Boss Wheel, Agapito, and the scouts ride up. Andrew and Christopher hold the reins of the crew's horses, and the men jump down to help heave the wagon. Agapito tells Larkin to help push while I drive the oxen.

Between five men and six oxen, they turn the wheels, just enough to move the wagon from the mud. Agapito shouts at me, "Do not let up, Dorcas. Keep them moving, and do not stop, yes?" I scream at the poor soggy beasts and crack the whip as tears stream down my cheeks, and icy rain pelts the rain gear. Over and over again, I whip the rain, trying to catch up to the wagon ahead.

Twice more, we become stuck, and it takes longer to dislodge the wagon each time. The unrelenting rain makes everything invisible, and I am surprised when the wagon in front of us finally comes to a halt. The wagons have circled, and I didn't even know we had reached our destination.

It is still pouring, and Larkin insists that the boys grease the axles. I plead with him to let the boys alone. "Climb in the wagon and rest. We need a break, Larkin."

"No, Dorcas. It doesn't matter how miserable or sick we are. We must take care of the wagon. I'll get the wagon jack." We share it between our five wagons, and since Stillman and Carter's wagon has the lightest load, they carry it in their rig.

Like everything else today, the task is more challenging than usual. The wagon jack sinks and tilts in the mushy earth. The boys place thick saplings underneath the jack and crank the wagon up enough to remove the wheels. Though they must be tired, they take the jack and muddy saplings to Cobb and Jennie's wagon and help them. Finally, Larkin and the boys return. I have nothing but hard biscuits, cold ham, and water for their supper. It is hard to cheer up a miserable family with cold food.

We're eager to get out of the rain, whereas Rose and Dahlia Jane have spent all day in the wagon. They are impatient to get out, even though it is wet.

I walk with the girls a short distance from the wagon to answer the call of nature. It is enough of a challenge as a lady, even under the best of circumstances. Typically, we would pay more attention to who might be watching or where we might be in relation to other people. Instead, we hurry when we should be careful.

After the girls finish, I attempt a squat. At the worst possible moment, my feet slip. I fall backward, and my naked rump lands in thick, squishy mud. I am unspeakably soiled and miserable to my core. I grit my teeth, trying not to complain. I'll have to go back to the wagon and get a towel.

Ten feet from the wagon stands a cross, fashioned out of tree branches, strapped together with twine where they join. A pile of earth and stones lay in front of the crude crucifix. The weathered sticks tilt slightly to the left. The dirt pile doesn't look large enough to be an adult's final resting place. I think of the poor traveling family that must have lost a child here. Perhaps it was last year. I say a quick prayer in my head and continue to the wagon. I turn to help Dahlia Jane up, and she's missing. Rose is gone too.

Doubling back, I find them standing beside the grave, hand in hand. The hood on Rose's raincoat rests on her back. Her head lolls forward, and her stringy wet hair dangles all about, obstructing the view of her face. I prod, "Come along, girls."

Rose drops Dahlia Jane's hand and waves me away without looking up. Rose sniffles as I rush the toddler away and lift her into the dry wagon. I rifle around, find a small towel, and shove it into the pocket of my skirt. Rose still stands beside the child's grave. I drape my arm across her shoulder, and she twists away from me. "I'm sorry, Rose. I know it is awful to imagine such a tragedy."

Larkin appears beside me with the boys.

Rose says, "Leave me alone," turning her back to us.

I turn toward Larkin and gesture toward Rose with open hands, imploring him to do something.

Larkin says, "Let her be. She'll learn to deal with the idea of death on her own. We all do, someday."

I protest. "I'm sure that Rose has many questions. I think we need to talk about this."

He responds, "This is not the time or place."

Rose turns halfway back toward us. She says, "I *don't* want to talk about it. I just want to be alone for a while."

Nevertheless, I step forward. Larkin raises his voice. "Let her be, Dorcas."

I want to shout back at him, but think better of it. I say, "Rose, honey. Let me know if you need me. I'm happy to listen if you want to talk."

Rose squats in front of the child's grave like she's about to warm her hands near a campfire. I look at Larkin. I have a sinking feeling in the pit of my stomach. My child needs something, I'm powerless to help her, and I haven't the slightest idea what's bothering her. It has been this way ever since she turned twelve.

Larkin points to the wagon with his chin, again telling me to leave Rose here, alone in the rain. I say, "I'll be along in a few minutes." Thick fog swallows me as I walk away from camp. I will not feel clean until I have a proper bath. I picture myself squatting on the prairie as I clean myself the best I can with a small towel and pray for an end to the rain.

When I return to camp, I see Rose waltzing about near the child's grave. She leans down and forward like she is dancing with an imaginary friend. I cover my mouth with my hand. I can't help thinking that Rose is losing her mind, and there's nothing I can do to stop it. Larkin says to ignore her. I know he's wrong, but I can't think of anything that will work, and every time I try, Rose pushes me further away. I back away toward the wagon and shiver, thinking of my poor child, obliviously dancing in the icy rain.

I climb into the back of the wagon, which was never intended to house a large family. We huddle inside, glad to be out of the rain, snuggling together under blankets.

It's hard to leave a child alone in the wilderness, exposed to the elements. I plead, "Larkin, Rose is out there, and I couldn't get her to come in. I don't know why she doesn't have the sense to come in out of the rain. I think you should go get her."

Larkin shakes his head in disagreement. In an even tone, he says, "I'm sure she will return soon. We can't let her ride in the wagon all day, even during bad weather. She'll come in when she gets cold enough. You can't coddle the children all the time, Dorcas."

Do all men say such things? I counter, "But Larkin, there's something wrong with Rose, isn't there? Can't you see that?" I don't want to say more with the other children listening.

Dismissively, he replies, "I'm sure it's just a phase she's going through. You mustn't worry so."

I pass out biscuits and dried apples. Dahlia Jane asks Larkin to read to her. Andrew scratches words onto lined paper. "I didn't get to post the news today, Mama. I'll have to post two issues tomorrow."

Larkin is right. Rose climbs into the wagon, dries her wet hair with a towel, and changes into her second dress beneath the cover of a blanket. Without a word to anyone, she begins writing in her diary. It has never occurred to me to read her private thoughts, but now I wonder whether I should.

As pitch-black darkness envelopes us, the children put their books away, close their eyes, and sleep. There isn't room for Larkin and me to stretch out, so we slump against each other and fall asleep slouched against our provisions. The corner of a wooden box presses into my back, and I can't seem to wriggle away from it.

Sleep comes in brief installments. The night seems as long as the day. I'm startled by a loud knocking on the side of the wagon. A man's voice shouts over the rain. "Larkin, it's your turn to take watch."

Larkin grumbles as he rises, puts on a raincoat, and disappears into the night. I feel sorry for him. Of all nights to have to stand watch. What can he see or prevent anyway? Then I feel guilty, enjoying the extra space, as

I stretch my body, wedge between warm, sleeping children, and fall fast asleep.

Wednesday, April 17

In the morning, I awaken before the trumpet sounds. Larkin hasn't returned, and my heart skips a beat when I see that Rose is gone as well.

Tinderbox in hand, I step off the wagon. There are a couple of dry sticks in the provision box attached to the wagon's side. When the fire catches, I look around for some wood to add to it.

Morning has almost dawned, and I wonder why the wagon masters haven't awakened us yet. Mercifully, the rain has stopped, and I am surprised to find a lovely grove of Elm trees. I walk a short distance into the woods and reach for a stick that looks dry enough to feed to the fire.

I'm startled to see Rose sitting on a rock beneath a tree. She turns her head one way, then the other. She looks like she's listening to a conversation between unseen companions. I glance about, and there isn't anybody here.

I rush back to the fire with sticks in my hands, wondering about Rose and whether hearing voices is one of the signs that somebody is going mad. What can we do but love her just the same? What if there is no way to prevent it? Will we just have to watch her get worse and worse? I shall have to think about the possibility.

My thoughts are interrupted, and I drop the wood I hold when the trumpet sounds. I'm glad I got a head start with my fire, and work as fast as possible to make pancakes. I send Andrew with a burning stick to the Banyon's camp to help them start a fire. Then, I dispatch Christopher to invite Stillman and Carter to breakfast with us.

Larkin appears, leading a pair of oxen. He looks like he has aged ten years in one night. It seems too soon for the demands of the journey to be so evident, but he doesn't look well rested. I flip a pancake and pour coffee into tin cups while Stillman and Carter leap forward to help Larkin harness the teams. Dahlia Jane and my boys join us around the fire, and Rose wanders in from the woods as if summoned by the smell of frying pancakes.

I wish we could spend the day in this pleasant, timbered grove, despite the eerie presence of a child's grave beside our wagon. I'm glad I prepared a double batch of batter as everyone seems to have an endless hunger this morning. It hasn't taken us long to learn to wolf breakfast, so we're ready to go in an hour.

Between mouthfuls, we discuss Bacon's bonnet mural. I ask Carter what he'd want, painted on their wagon cover. He removes his hat, shakes his hair back, though it isn't very long, and answers. "Maybe the ocean. When we get to Oregon, I'd like to see the waves crashing onto the shore. Perhaps he could paint that."

It seems strange to me. I would imagine painting things we might see along the way, not something we'll never encounter. But, it's nice to hear the polite young man offer an opinion on something, and it would be nice to see the ocean. I say, "That's nice, Carter." I remove the last pancake from the skillet and ask Stillman what he would have painted on the wagon cover.

He grimaces, raises an eyebrow, and rubs his behind. "Certainly not a hive of bees. Got stung yesterday. Raised a massive welt. Hurts to sit down. Gotta warn ya, don't get too close to that fellow, Schuyler Steele's wagon.

It's full of bees. He doesn't seem to care about marching along with a swarm, but I couldn't do it. Good thing we don't have to travel next to him. So, I surely wouldn't want to paint anything on the wagon that would appeal to bees."

Instead of hearing what Stillman wouldn't want, I'd rather know what he would have, but time is wasting and chores won't wait. I suppose it doesn't matter. I fancy the notion that Bacon will paint everyone's wagon bonnets, but why should he? He'll probably be tired at the end of the day and have more practical concerns, but if he offers, I'd love to have him decorate our wagon.

With breakfast over, Stillman and Carter rush off to yoke their oxen. Rose milks the goat, and Dahlia Jane rips clumps of grass from the ground for Gloria, the caged hen. Dahlia Jane asks Rose if she could make a halter for the chicken and use a rope so she can take the bird for walks during the day. Though it sounds frivolous, I encourage them. Perhaps it will do them good to busy themselves with such an activity.

As we roll away from the pretty campground that we hardly had a chance to enjoy, Rose walks backward as if she's watching someone behind us. I look back but don't see anything except for a string of wagons, one dutifully following another. I look at Rose again, and her head twists and turns as if she's watching something that clearly isn't there.

An hour later, it's still cloudy, and it looks like it could rain again. When I mention it to Andrew, he says, "No, Mama. It isn't going to rain today."

My head slowly shakes back and forth. That boy is a constant amazement. I inquire, "How do you always know?"

He shrugs. "I don't know, Mama. I just know. Mark my words. Let's see if I am right."

After a while, Agapito rides up. He tells us about the parting of the trails, which is almost upon us. Though he's mostly talking to Andrew, I hang on his words, enjoying the sound of his voice. The route to Santa Fe will lead to the southwest, and we'll continue to the northwest. He looks across the prairie. I wonder what he's thinking and mirror his movements. It's hard to have a sense of direction on a cloudy day, but Agapito looks away from the trail to the southwest and tells us not to worry. All we need to do is follow the wagon in front of us, but he thought Andrew might want to mention the landmark in his newspaper. Agapito compliments Andrew on his latest issue, and then rides off to visit Stillman and Carter.

The muddy trail slows the oxen, and after plodding along on foot for a few hours, it is understandable that we should move more slowly. It takes extra effort to lift our feet from the muddy ground as a fair measure of thick muck clings to our boots. I'm constantly lifting my skirts to keep the hem from gathering pounds of dirt from the ground, at the risk of exposing my underpinnings.

Larkin is irritable. I know that he suffers from a lack of sleep, so I struggle to keep from arguing with him. I silently listen as he complains for an hour about the muddy trail. By mid-morning, Larkin says, "I feel dizzy. I think I got the seasickness again."

"How can you have seasickness on dry land?"

Larkin shivers and shrugs. "I think I'm going to vomit."

I'm sure that he is being dramatic. Instead of arguing, I remain silent. When he begins to moan, I say, "Let me lead the teams."

He hands me the whip and scampers off onto the prairie. I feel bad for the poor beasts, having to drag our home down the muddy trail. When I look back, Larkin has fallen to his prayer bones. I chastise myself for not being more sympathetic and hope he isn't retching. He will have to take care of himself. I must keep the wagon rolling. I glance back again, then look toward the boys.

Andrew says, "I'll take the bullwhip, Mama."

"Thank you, Andrew. We must keep them going so that we don't get stuck."

"I know. Don't worry, Mama."

Poor Andrew. It's not his turn to walk with Hardtack, Scrapple, and the rest of the oxen, but I'm worried about Larkin. Maybe if I were prone to seasickness, I wouldn't have been so callous.

Leaving Andrew with the wagon, I dash off toward Larkin. He has regained his feet, but his legs seem wobbly again. His breath smells sour, and I refrain from looking at the grass where he kneeled. I tell him, "Hold on to my arm, dear." We walk slowly back toward the wagon. It takes an hour to catch up to our place in line. I feel like I'm walking with a grandparent rather than my husband. I say, "I want you to lie down in the wagon."

Larkin doesn't argue, but it takes a great effort to move him fast enough to push him up into the back of the rolling wagon.

As the day goes on, the trail gets dryer. The oxen plod along, only bellowing a complaint now and then. We drag our mudhooks across the prairie, and I'm sure the children are looking forward to taking a break as much as we are.

When I check on Larkin and Dahlia Jane in the wagon, she is reciting a fable to him. Perhaps it is one of the stories he reads to her while I prepare dinner. I hear a low moan coming from Larkin, but it doesn't bother Dahlia Jane, so I leave them as they are.

Finally, I'm relieved to see the wagons ahead begin to form a circle. Andrew, Christopher, and I unyoke the team. Rose builds a fire and then milks the goat. Then Andrew posts his newspaper at The Hub. I ask Christopher to invite the Banyons to join us for supper.

As I turn toward the wagon ahead of us, Agapito rides forward, and the Indian scouts ride alongside him. Agapito says, "Arikta shot a mule deer today."

The scout hands me a couple of pounds of meat. I look at him and thank him as my stomach grinds eagerly.

Agapito says, "A little bit of stew will do everybody good, no?" As he rides away, I'm glad we joined a company that occasionally provides fresh meat to its passengers.

My sharp paring knife makes quick work of the venison, as I dice the meat into cubes and set the skillet onto the fire's edge. Then, I help Larkin climb down from the wagon. His skin looks gray, like the ashes in a fire that's gone cold. "Are you feeling any better? Did riding in the wagon help?"

Larkin groans. "I don't think so. I think riding makes it worse. I feel like a sailor, lost in a tempestuous sea. Every little pebble tosses one around. I think it would be better to walk. At least you can see the horizon at the edge of the sea."

"You mean at the edge of the prairie?"

"That's what I said, isn't it?"

I lie and resist the urge to roll my eyes. "Of course, silly me."

I remove a couple of boxes of provisions from the wagon and lower Larkin onto one of them. He sits forward, props his elbows on his legs, and sets his chin in his hands.

When the Banyons arrive, Jennie groans as we lower her onto a box next to Larkin. I turn to the fire, thicken the stew with flour, and add spices to the pot.

I'm surprised to see Rose has already finished making a harness for the chicken. Christopher holds the small crate open while Rose dresses the bird and ties the lead to the halter. The fluffy yellow chicks protest as the child lifts Gloria from the cage. Rose hands Dahlia Jane the leash and watches as the hen parades around the campground, pecking dirt like she is making up for missed meals.

The empty cage reveals a fresh egg. I wrap it in a small piece of fabric and set it into the top of a box of oats, which will cushion the egg as we travel and keep it from breaking. Christopher places the handful of growing chicks in an empty box and dumps the soiled contents of the cage on the other side of the wagon. I ask Christopher if he can find something for the bottom of the enclosure as I set it back on its shelf, but I should just let him tend the flock. He seems to know just what animals need without being told, and has made it a point to look in on our poultry frequently.

I pour coffee for Larkin and Cobb, and stir weak lemonade for the rest of us. I can't help thinking of Agapito's cologne as I mix water, sugar, and extract. Jennie empties a cup like she hasn't had anything to drink all day, and I pour her a second helping. I ask, "Are you drinking enough during the day, dear?"

Jennie sighs, and says, "I do the best I can to keep up." Everything about the woman is delicate, including her spoken words and the breaths she takes.

Cobb's brow furrows. "You keep up just fine. We need to make sure you rest more, though."

The woman places a hand on my forearm. Her touch is so gentle and ladylike, I can't help being concerned. Jennie says, "Mr. Banyon worries too much and always spoils me terribly." The woman's loving gaze locks onto the man she married, as if her life depends on watching him, and then she hums, ever so quietly.

I tell Cobb to make sure and let me know whenever there's something I can do to help.

Without looking away from Cobb, Jennie blinks, gently rubs her belly, and say's, "We'll be fine. Cobb always says, 'One at a time.' If we take one day at a time, before we know it, we'll be in Oregon. If we take one step at a time, we'll make it through the day."

"Your husband is a wise man," I say. I wonder about her previous pregnancies, and would like to ask whether they were as hard on her as this one seems to be, but decide to ask her the next time we're alone together. I add, "The trail has been hard on Larkin, too."

My husband frowns but doesn't reply. He's managed to eat a few bites. Jennie glances at him quickly, then says to me, "We have been worried about Larkin. I wish there was something we could do to help."

Cobb optimistically says, "I'm sure that tomorrow will be better."

It isn't raining, and I have a good fire going. I'd rather visit with friends or watch the children play, but I had better make more biscuits in case it starts raining again. Chores don't stop just because we have company in camp. I push my sleeves up to my elbows and glance at my muscular, unladylike forearms as I vigorously stir the batter, leaving the conversation to others. I imagine a future in which women will have machines to help with such work. There's plenty of women like Jennie that could use all the help they could get. I should be content that I have a Dutch oven in which to cook biscuits.

After supper, our friends retreat to their wagon, and I send them off with a quart of goat's milk and a small basket of biscuits for their breakfast.

The boys pitch the tent, the girls prepare for bed, and then, Larkin and the boys check on the stock. While they're away, the Committeemen and their wives pass through camp.

Captain Meadows asks how we're doing, and I tell him about Larkin's seasickness. He says a prayer for Larkin and looks about our camp like he's making an inspection. I like his wife, a pretty woman named Luella, who looks to be my age.

Travis and Catherine Latham are a handsome couple, younger than the Meadows. When Captain Meadows introduces them to me, I say, "How do you do?"

Travis moans, "I have a gruesome toothache, and I swear it's going to be the death of me."

Catherine quips, "Travis is like a bear with a thorn in his paw. I don't know why he doesn't just get it pulled. Don't worry none about him."

Next, Reverend Meadows introduces Wade and Dottie Crouse. They don't say much until it is time to leave. As they move toward the next wagon, Dottie grips my forearm and whispers, "I hear the way you argue with your husband. You really should hold your tongue, Mrs. Moon. It isn't right to pester a man so."

I smile politely, thank her for her concern, and tell her I will try to remember that. I hope that The Committee will not favor us with too many such visits.

After getting my family settled for the night, I make my way to the estuary named Captain Creek. There's barely enough light in the cloudy sky by which to see. I'm sure Dottie Crouse would disapprove of a woman stepping out alone after dark.

I walk a short distance downstream, look quickly about and drop my dirty dress on the ground. I remove my corset and set it on top of my clothes. I shiver as I shed my sweaty shift and step into the frigid water. I take a deep breath and submerge all at once, up to my chin, careful not to get my hair wet. Removing the unwelcome mud from my nether regions with a washcloth is a Heavenly feeling, despite the icy bath. As soon as I feel clean, I step back onto the riverbank. A cold breeze chills my skin as

I towel off. It feels good to put on clean clothes. Now I can't wait to get back to the wagon and, hopefully, a good night's sleep.

As I tiptoe back toward camp, I hear a distant howling. My body trembles at the thought of being alone in the wilderness, surrounded by wolves. My pace quickens. My dirty dress and wet towel are tucked at my side, by my elbow. I lean forward, and peer into the darkness, first to the left and then to the right. Then, I look back to my left again.

The sight of two pairs of eyes, one slightly higher than the other, forces me to gasp. Without a doubt, the fiery white orbs are the eyeshine of wolves, like the ones in my nightmares. I start to run, and crash into a man.

He is young, handsome, and muscular. I look up into his eyes, realizing that he is taller than I am, by at least several inches. He says, "Howdy, ma'am, my name is Alvah——Alvah Nye. I hope that I didn't frighten you."

My words are slow to form, which is seldom a problem for me. Finally, I croak, "I know I shouldn't be out after dark, but I just had to freshen up." Then, my words spill out more quickly. "Oh, Heaven's sakes. Pardon my manners. I'm Dorcas Moon, Mrs. Dorcas Moon, wagon number sixteen." I look down beside him and jump back in surprise. A big black dog sits loyally beside him.

"Don't be frightened, Mrs. Moon. Unless you are a duck, you have nothing to worry about. May I present Miss Honey Nye, wagon number thirty-one."

I gulp. "I'm sorry, Mr. Nye. I like to think I am a brave woman, but I've always been afraid of dogs for some reason——dogs and wolves, that is."

Alvah bends at the waist and pats the dog's head. "Well, Mrs. Moon, I suppose everybody's afraid of something, and some people are afraid of everything. But I hope you'll give Honey a chance to befriend you."

Rather than focus on the canine, I address the man. "I'm sorry, Mr. Nye. Please call me Dorcas."

Ever so slightly, his shoulders tip forward, as if to indicate a courteous bow. "That's very kind of you. You must return the favor and call me Alvah. May I escort you back to your wagon, Dorcas?"

Tentatively, my head sways, neither shaking or nodding, and then I consent. "Yes. I'm afraid that after my ablutions, I heard howling wolves and saw two pairs of eyeballs at the river just before I crashed into you."

Alvah turns his head, not fearfully, but with interest. He acknowledges, "Eyeshine. Whatever you saw couldn't be too far away." Honey looks off toward the river as if she knows what we're talking about and where the creatures are. "We best get you back to camp."

Alvah offers me his arm. I grab hold like I'm being chased by wolves, then let up. "I'm sorry, Alvah. The thought of wolves has me on edge."

He laughs in a reassuring manner. "You didn't hurt me."

Men are supposed to be stronger than women, but I could beat most of them at arm wrestling. I don't think I'd have a chance at besting Alvah Nye, whose arms are as solid as tree trunks. If I were fifteen years younger, we'd make quite a couple. Why must I think such thoughts?

When we reach the campground, I thank Alvah for seeing me safely home. Then, I hang my wet towel on a peg on the other side of the wagon. Whether it's the darkness or my absentmindedness, I trip on a tent stake and crash to the ground. My hands catch my fall.

I shake my head in disappointment. A good bath doesn't last very long in the wilderness.

Thursday, April 18

Will I ever get used to Agapito's blasted trumpet? For a moment, I ponder, trying to remember where we are. Then, I recall Captain Creek, my nocturnal bathing, and the good-looking young man that escorted me home.

As I climb from the wagon with my tinderbox, I think about the decent man I married and our blessed family. I harken back to Noah, the boy I loved so desperately as a young girl, and sometimes, I grieve the loss of something I never possessed. The way that Jennie looks at Cobb comes to my mind. With a wistful sigh, I remember the strong arm of the tall man beside the river. Then I think of the gallant, slender man on the golden mare. Finally, I look into the gaunt face of a familiar man with a hangdog mustache, which normally is fully waxed, parallel to his shoulders.

I query, "Are you feeling any better today, Larkin?"

He breathes deeply, looks around camp, and exhales. "I think so. Maybe I just needed a good night's sleep." Larkin clasps my elbow in his hand and kisses me briefly before stumbling off to fetch a team of oxen.

It's only our fourth morning on the trail, and it seems like we've been traveling for months. We don't need to think about the tasks anymore. They're already performed ritually.

The weather is mostly cloudy, but dry. We walk, hour after hour. I'm careful not to think of it as dull, especially compared to that rainy day when we trudged through the wagon-eating mud. The oxen seem content to walk a dry path.

We have decided that Andrew and Christopher shall drive the oxen. Dahlia Jane must walk whenever possible, but she can take frequent breaks in the wagon. Rose must walk as well. Agapito has challenged us to lighten our load, and his warnings set fire to a nagging doubt I carry in the pit of my stomach. What if the wagon master or his crew discovers Larkin's heavy safe?

Our scouts have found a place where the grass has grown tall enough for grazing. Nothing seems to stop my stomach from growling at me, yet when we stop for a meal, I decide that I'm not that hungry, once I begin eating. As I stir a pot of beans and fry bacon, I decide to surprise my family with a cake to go with supper tonight.

After dinner at mid-day, Andrew walks forward to conduct interviews while Christopher leads the team. When he returns, he sits in the wagon for an hour and prepares today's bulletin. I walk at the back of the wagon while he works. Sometimes he asks me how to spell a word. I'm not sure whether I know the correct answers. He's a better speller than I am, despite his age.

In the distance, I see a small bump of a hill. I can't take my eyes off the incline after days of walking a trail so flat that it may as well be a wooden board. I'm not especially homesick, but I miss the mountains that dominate the landscape back home. The distant hill seems to beckon us forward, calling us to it, yet it always seems just beyond reach.

Andrew makes a quick note of the knoll at the bottom of the page, and then he says that he is finished. I ask about the weather, and he says, "No rain today, and no rain tomorrow."

We pass the beautiful hill and reach a small, wooded river during the afternoon. It seems a little earlier than most afternoons, and I'm glad the wagons are circling. I should spend the extra time scrubbing clothes, but instead, I saddle Blizzard.

I ride toward the river, and the stallion takes a short drink. I doff my bonnet and unbraid my hair. Then, we cross, and I guess this is where the wagons will ford the river tomorrow morning. On the other side, I squeeze my legs, loosen my hold on the reins, and let Blizzard run. I turn him to the left, and we race toward the west. From a slightly higher point on the prairie, to the north of the river, I see the winding path that the river takes. I ride back at a slow, loping canter and enjoy Blizzard's gentle, rocking rhythm.

A loud pop explodes in the air.

I pull the reins tight, and Blizzard's hind legs drag to a stop. Two more shots ring out. The bang sounds are so loud they must come from a nearby gun. Then, there is silence.

Cautiously, I ride toward the river, and see somebody there. I squint, trying to figure out who it is. It's not the scouts from our wagon train. I can make out a man, and something bouncing around him. I ride closer and realize it is the man from last night and his dog, Honey.

It is never a good idea to sneak up on a man with guns, so I ride up slowly. I call out, "Alvah! Alvah Nye. It's Dorcas. Dorcas Moon." As I approach, he throws his hands up like I'm going to arrest him, and then I realize he is showing me something. I squeeze my legs, and Blizzard lopes toward Alvah. Honey sits at his side, and Alvah holds three ducks by their webbed feet.

Alvah shouts, "Want one?"

When I reach him, I answer, "Sure. Why don't you join us for supper? I'd like you to meet my family."

He nods, once, and tips his hat back with the business end of his shotgun. "It would be an honor and a pleasure."

Alvah steps aboard a big bay horse he calls Monsoon, and we cross the river together. I look back and see Honey's snout above the water's surface, paddling behind us. Alvah says, "She loves to swim." I laugh when the dog shakes after she finishes crossing.

When we reach the other side of the river, I ask Alvah if he minds letting Andrew interview him for the newspaper.

He looks surprised. Most people are never asked to answer a journalist's questions. "I suppose that'd be alright."

I *thought* the family would like the young man, but I'm surprised to discover how quickly Christopher, in particular, takes to Alvah. The boy says, "You shot three ducks at once?"

With a slow drawl, Alvah confirms, "Yes, I guess I did. Not with one shot, mind you."

Christopher stomps a foot, which is just one of the ways my enthusiastic son indicates he's impressed. "Will you give me lessons? Can I go hunting with you sometime?"

Alvah glances at me. "Well, we'll see. I'll have to talk to your parents about that first, but how would you like to help me get them cleaned up so we can make a meal of them?" Alvah removes his hat, swings his straight brown hair back into place, and puts his hat back on his head.

I interrupt. "There's a lot of meat on these plump ducks. Do you mind if I invite our neighbors in the next wagon?"

He shakes his head. "Of course not. I'm happy to share. I only wish I could feed everyone."

I chuckle. "Perhaps you shall, before we reach Oregon."

Alvah drives y-shaped sticks into the ground beside the fire, skewers the ducks, and leaves them to roast while I make my way to the next wagon.

I don't see Stillman and Carter, so I glance around. Then I step up and peek into their wagon. I'm shocked to see them locked in an embrace and kissing passionately, like a man and woman.

My heart pounds, and I blurt out, "I'm sorry. I'm sorry to interrupt. I shouldn't have violated your privacy." I pause awkwardly and then continue. "We have ducks roasting over the fire, more than we can eat, and we'd like to have you join us for dinner."

I jump away from the wagon, start back toward our camp, and then turn around. I hear the boys' urgent whispering, but I can't discern their words. Returning to their wagon, I whisper loud enough so that only they can hear me, and they instantly become silent. I say, "What I saw is none of my business. I will not tell a soul. Don't be angry with me. Please come to supper."

I hear a tentative, high-pitched squeak. Perhaps it's Stillman. He says, "Yes, ma'am."

In what I hope is a regular voice, I say. "Good. It's settled then."

My stomach feels like it is in my throat. I've never seen anything that shocked me more. I've heard sermons about such things, but I've never known anyone to whom those sermons might apply, and nobody I know has either.

I walk as slowly as I can. I wish I had time to think. Does this change how I feel about Stillman? Or Carter? They don't seem like sinners to me. I should be horrified by what I saw. I should warn everyone else about them. Instead, I just want to wrap my arms around them and hug them tightly, pressing them closer together. I try to shake the picture of them from my mind, but it is burned brightly into my memory. They look cherubic, and I firm my resolve to protect them like a mother bear protects her cubs, for if anyone discovers their secret, their lives could be ruined. They might even be killed.

So what if most of the world thinks that they should be banished or condemned. Even when I was listening in church, I never put much stock in thoughts of a vengeful God. Jesus taught acceptance and forgiveness, and that's good enough for me, yet, still, I can't look directly into their eyes when they approach our fire. Their cheeks look sunburned, and I can imagine they are blushing with embarrassment, knowing that I saw them. I hope they aren't afraid of what I will say. I have not been very good at keeping secrets during my life, but I am determined to keep theirs. I shudder to think of what might happen if somebody else discovered them. They shall have to be more careful in the future.

"Alvah Nye, I'd like you to meet our neighbors, Stillman Southmaid and Carter Wilson." My eyes flutter as I continue, and wonder whether their familial claim is true. "They're cousins from our hometown, in northern New York. Where are you from, Alvah?"

"I'm from Cumberland, Maryland. This is my girl, Honey. We're hunters." Alvah extends his hand, first to Stillman and then to Carter. "Glad to meet you." If he senses Stillman and Carter's hesitation, it is not apparent.

I ask Andrew and Christopher to get more boxes from the wagon, and Alvah follows them. I stick a knife in one of the roasting ducks. Fat spurts out and crackles into the fire. Alvah returns carrying three boxes and asks if he can help me. "I was going to carve them on this board," I answer. Before I can object, Alvah is hard at work, slicing up the birds.

My heart aches for Stillman and Carter. Carter's eyes scarcely leave the fire, though he tends to be reserved anyway. Stillman looks at his hands, and all I can think of is Lady Macbeth, but Stillman hasn't murdered anybody. There's no reason he should feel like a criminal. I try to make light conversation with them, but nothing cuts through the fog of awkwardness that envelopes us tonight.

After supper, I surprise everyone with the cake I baked at noon. The icing isn't as good as I made back home, but it's the best cake we've had on the prairie. The children are delighted, and the adults also clean their plates.

Alvah says, "I'd better get back to my place. First, I want to stop and read today's news. My place is directly across the circle from yours. Stop by anytime."

Stillman says, "We'd better go as well."

I assert, "I'll walk back with you."

His head pitches forward. "Yes, ma'am."

I notice Larkin's eyebrows raise. Stillman hasn't called us sir or ma'am in a while.

When we arrive beside their wagon, I say, "I meant what I said. Your secret is safe with me, and I'll love you as much tomorrow as I did yesterday."

Stillman looks directly into my eyes. "You love us?"

"Yes, Stillman. I always have, and I always will." I stretch my arms and sweep them into an embrace. I'm sure I'm smothering them, but I don't care. I'll hold them until they're ready to part, as long as it takes. Carter sniffles, then peels away first. Stillman tips his head back and gazes at me with his dark, wet eyes.

He drops his head and steps away. He turns around briefly and whispers, "We're not really cousins, but I guess you've figured that out."

Its a relief to know, and I'm glad Stillman told me without making me ask. I sympathize, "I understand."

Stillman quickly whispers, "Thank you, Dorcas," and hurries to follow Carter into the wagon.

I nod and turn back toward camp. As I clean the dishes and prepare for bed, I think about Stillman and Carter. In the distance, a wolf howls, and I shiver. Why must they do that when the rest of the world is quiet?

Friday, April 19

My eyeballs rattle when the trumpet blasts me from the wagon at three, like a nightmare that happens over and over again.

I peek through the hole at the back of the wagon and see darkness, but I don't see rain. I think about everything that happened yesterday, and I'm amazed that it was just one day, merely a speck of dust in an endless desert.

After building my fire, I tiptoe backward through the darkness until I hear men talking from the wagon master's camp. I admonish myself for being a busybody, and rationalize that I'm within the bounds of our camp. Boss Wheel speaks in his regular, gravelly voice. "She is a little high but crossable. We are lucky. Reckon we'll lose any pilgrims today?"

The scouts grumble answers that aren't reassuring. Agapito says, "Something bad always happens during our first crossing, yes? Today we must do better."

Boss Wheel snorts, "I hope God listens to Captain Meadows' prayers this morning." The way he says it, I'm not sure whether it is God or Captain Meadows that Boss Wheel disbelieves.

I slither back to my morning chores. All around me, I can hear the deafening silence that follows Reveille, followed by a building din of noise as emigrants awaken and face a new day. Everything on the wagon train makes noise. Today, like every other, begins with banging dishes and rattling pans, followed by bellowing oxen and braying mules, rattling chains, and chattering people. If today is different, it is because of a river crossing.

Agapito rides into camp and says, "We cross the Wakarusa River this morning."

I ask about the hill that we passed yesterday.

He extends an arm in the direction of the landmark, as if formally introducing it. "That's Blue Mound."

"Oh." Many of the Oregon Trail's landmarks, like Alcove Springs, are famous, having been mentioned in newspapers across the country, but I don't recall ever having heard of Blue Mound. But the river crossing is more important than hillsides. I think of our friends from home and the fears they haven't hesitated to mention frequently. I implore, "Agapito, would you look after the Bull family? Addie is petrified, and I don't think he'd want to tell you, but I believe Pious is scared too."

He nods, and I'm sure he will spend extra time with the Bull family. He reassures, "A good drover does not need to worry. Keep the teams moving. Do not slow down. It is hesitation that gets us in trouble at the Wakarusa. Make sure you crack that whip. Make all the noise you can, yes?"

The river didn't look scary when I crossed it riding Blizzard yesterday, and it doesn't look frightening today either. Maybe crossing rivers with a wagon isn't the same as walking or riding a horse across. I think about the river current hitting the side of the wagon.

We watch as the first wagon crosses. Instead of riding directly across, the wagon zigs down current to the halfway point and zags up the river before it climbs the bank safely to the other side.

As the second wagon crosses, I say to Larkin, "I want you to walk the children across. Would you do this for me?" His skin looks almost green, like the very thought of riding the wagon across the river makes him seasick.

He asks me, "Are you worried?"

I confidently shake my head. "If you carry Dahlia Jane, no. I will not worry."

He frowns. Is he thinking about the heavy safe in the wagon? He says, "I don't know, Dorcas. I'm afraid that you will not crack the whip."

I assure Larkin that I have learned my lesson and remind him that I can shout louder than he can.

He says, "That's for certain. I can attest to that." He manages a mild grin, tips his head, and looks up at me with an arched eyebrow. He doesn't say it, but I think he is grateful.

Ten wagons safely cross ahead of us. I watch as Larkin carries Dahlia Jane into the water, followed by Rose leading the angry goat. The boys scamper across the river, playfully, behind them.

Then, it is my turn. Though I hadn't been nervous earlier, doubt gnaws in my gut.

I mutter, "Please forgive me, Hardtack. And Scrapple." I crack the whip and shout at the oxen in front of me. As they pull the wagon into the river, I wish they were moving faster.

I crack the whip furiously, but the team can barely pull the wagon. It sounds like somebody is throwing rocks at the wagon. I glance into the water and see floating chunks of ice. I yell at the oxen like I'm shouting at the Devil, though I just want to throw my arms around their necks and weep for them. Instead, I snap the bullwhip all about them furiously, as if their lives depend on it.

When we finally reach the middle of the river, the scout standing in the water directs me to turn the team toward the riverbank. I scream like a crazy woman and beg the team to pull harder against the current.

Finally, when the team stands, heaving with exhaustion, on the other side of the river, Agapito shouts up to me. "Good job, Dead Aim Dorcas.

But it should be easier than that, yes? Your wagon is too heavy. You must lighten the load." Then, he returns to the riverbank to guide the next wagon ashore.

I climb down, turn the oxen over to the boys, and collapse on the ground. "I need to rest for a few minutes." Sitting near the riverbank, I watch as Stillman and Carter emerge from the river. Their oxen don't seem tired at all. They aren't pulling a heavy iron safe, or a cookstove, all the way to Oregon.

Carter's hand slaps the top of his head, and he glances about like he's looking for something he misplaced. He must have lost his hat in the river.

Across the river, I see Jennie seated on a box in the wagon, watching Cobb drive their oxen. I wish someone could carry her across the river, just as Larkin cradled Dahlia Jane. Cobb's oxen have no trouble pulling the wagon downstream until Agapito starts shouting from the riverbank. "Log in the river."

His warning comes too late. Arikta, the scout, directs Cobb to maneuver against the current toward the riverbank, and just as Cobb turns the team, the floating log smacks into the side of his wagon. I jump to my feet, screaming.

The impact rocks the wagon, but it doesn't tip. Cobb desperately climbs into the wagon and grabs Jennie. One fast splash follows another. First, Bess lands, splashing in the water, and then Joe. Boss Wheel grabs Bess, pitches her onto his shoulder, and trudges toward the shore. But where is Joe?

I shout. "There's a little boy, also." I jump up and down, screaming. "Somebody save Joe Banyon." My feet start moving, and I find myself running, madly, back toward the river.

The scout hollers at Cobb's oxen.

Cobb and Jennie look into the river, trying to find Joe.

A little way down the river, I see splashing, and run toward the commotion. It's amazing how quickly the current has carried Joe along. Alvah Nye follows Honey into the water and scoops the boy into the crook of his arm. The child looks so small in the big man's arms. It takes a couple of moments for me to reach Alvah's side. He hands Joe to me, and I stare for a moment, amazed to see the child's unworried face. Alvah places his big hand on my shoulder for half a second, and then he splashes off to help Cobb and Jennie down from the wagon.

Joe looks into my eyes. His body shivers compulsively, and his teeth chatter. His bright white eyes glimmer, and he says, "That was fun. Do it again!" I wrap my arms around the imp and pull him into my bosom, trying to warm him up while Jennie and Cobb attempt to calm his wailing sister.

Agapito clears the riverbank to prepare for the next wagon's crossing.

When it is Pious and Addie Bull's turn, my friend stands in front of their wagon, back to the river, blocking the wagon's progress. She screams, "No, we're not going. I can't do it. It isn't safe. Let's go back."

Without thinking, I pass Joe to Cobb and splash across the river. Halfway across, it registers just how cold the water is. I surprise Addie from behind. Before she realizes what's happening, I'm holding her in my arms like a new bride crossing the threshold.

"Put me down. Why, Dorcas! What do you think you're doing? No, I'm not going to cross that river."

She doesn't even realize she's already halfway across. I try to keep her body above the surface, but her skirts drag the water around my waist. I stumble and almost drop her. She screams, and I'm sure her rear end must be submerged. It can't be helped. She sobs angry tears as I haul her body up the riverbank and set her to stand, looking back upon the river, as Pious drives their team through the Wakarusa River.

Lloyd and Hetty Carpenter and their three young daughters in wagon number five are the last to emerge from the river. Agapito shouts triumphantly, "Everyone has made it safely across. The Wakarusa was no match for us today." Despite the dramatic crossing, Carter's hat is the only casualty of the day. "Change into dry clothes, *mis amigos*. We have a long day ahead of us, yes?"

On overcast days, wildflowers dazzle, even more than when the sun shines brightly, and contrast with the lush green grasses. The cheerful flora turns my head, and my mind cartwheels across the prairie, frolicking in the splendor. Vibrant clusters of bell-shaped, Virginia bluebells wash across the prairie. They contrast with occasional clumps of bright, pink prairie mallow. The sweet scent of wild blue phlox is delightful, and fuzzy, pink and white pussytoes add texture to the landscape.

With nine blasts of the trumpet, we're on the move again. Despite the change of clothes, the air is cool, and the sky is cloudy. I ask Andrew for an update on the weather. I don't know how he does it. I can't remember the last time that he was wrong. He insists that it will not rain today. "Tomorrow is another story."

After supper, I wander onto the prairie, beyond the mineral springs, with the girls, looking for a likely place to tempt a snake. That's a euphemism of our own making.

We make our way around a tree, and I hear a low, growling sound. I stop, frozen in place, and pull Dahlia Jane and Rose to my side with a gasp.

Three, green-eyed wolves tug a human carcass apart. A shallow grave a few feet away did nothing to protect a man in his final resting place. I gulp a breath of air down my windpipe and cover the girls' eyes with my hands.

My feet come alive beneath me, and I edge backward as Rose bends her head away from my hand. I make a hushing sound as we retreat. I feel myself trembling and wish I could be braver.

Back at the encampment, I leave the girls with Larkin and head for the wagon master's camp. My composure gives way to rare tears. I can't keep my cheeks dry despite wiping my face with my hand. "Agapito, there's a dead man, yanked from his eternal slumber and dismembered by a pack of wolves." I can't speak of it anymore.

He grabs a shovel from the side of his wagon, picks up his rifle, and checks the gun in his holster. He says, "You must try to forget what you have seen, Dorcas."

I nod and wonder if it is possible to forget such a thing. I watch as Agapito and his scout follow my finger into the gloaming in search of the shredded corpse. Our friends need to know about the dangerous wolves, and we must stick together.

I return to our wagon to get the girls. Rose yelps as I grab her hand. It's hard to be gentle when you are afraid for your life. I try to make up for it by taking Dahlia Jane's hand gently in my own. We make our way to Jennie's wagon, then Esther's, and finally Addie's.

Sometimes modesty is a luxury we cannot afford. We walk together a short distance from the wagons, making a circle standing with our backs to each other, ankle to ankle. We take turns tempting snakes within the ring, answering nature's call in the middle, under the cover of our skirts, held wide in our hands.

When it is finally time to go to sleep, Dahlia Jane shivers at my side, complaining about the darkness surrounding us. She is afraid. I wonder if

Rose is troubled as well, though she says she is fine. I make up a long, gentle story about people with cat faces, the kind Dahlia Jane can't get enough of. I surmise that Rose has fallen asleep by the sound of her breathing. Eventually, Dahlia Jane lulls into slumber as well.

I wish that someone would whack me in the head with a shovel. I can't get the thought of those slobbering wolves chomping on that poor man's flesh and bones out of my head.

Saturday, April 20

At the sound of Reveille, I jump as if from a deep sleep, though I don't believe I slept a wink. I was too afraid that I might dream of wolves eating my family, like they did that poor man last night.

Howling winds and driving rain battered the wagon's bonnet above us, all night long. At midnight, Larkin passed the boys through the tiny opening behind the wagon and climbed aboard after them.

Rose is awake, and she says, "That man is dead, and his spirit is in Heaven. He can't feel anything." I'm surprised that Rose is trying to comfort me and that she seems unafraid.

I say, "Thank you, dear. That's a comfort to hear." But it isn't. How would she know the condition of that man's poor, tortured soul? I wonder what killed him, but I can't imagine his demise was worse than the desecration of his grave.

With a groan, I rise and put on my rain gear. I shake Larkin and hand him his India rubber. "I'll help you harness the teams." Thunder claps in the sky above us as I give each child a biscuit. The wind forces the cold rain sideways, peppering our faces. Larkin is right beside me. "I predict it is going to be a long day. At least tomorrow is a day of rest. I think we're going to need it."

Despite the mud, we stop for dinner at mid-day. There's no chance of a fire. The children complain of boredom, and despite my protests, Larkin insists that the children drive the oxen during the afternoon.

We reach our destination late in the afternoon. It has stopped raining, but the wind still howls. Like the rest of the emigrants, I search for dry wood along the wide, muddy Kaw River. It makes the mighty Wakarusa River seem like a babbling brook in comparison.

I fight the winds that conspire against me as I attempt to light a fire. Everyone hungers for a hot and hearty meal tonight.

Agapito comes to my rescue with a torch from the fire beside his wagon. I thank him, and ask whether we will cross tomorrow or the next day. He tells me that he thinks it will be tomorrow. As he sets out with his torch to assist other passengers, I ask him to tell Stillman and Carter to join us.

Everyone hunches over steaming plates of bacon and beans, huddled together to keep the wind at our backs. We barely manage a few bites when we are interrupted by a piercing scream.

I spring to my feet and see a woman running toward us from across the ring of wagons. Her skirts are ablaze. She spins as she runs, screaming, and I run toward her. Others reach the woman just as I do, and she falls to the ground, writhing in pain. The fire from her dress spreads into the grass around her, dry despite the rain, and radiates.

Leon Humphries says, "That's Bridget Sawyer. She drug the bottom of her dress through her campfire. I saw it happen. Her wagon is next to mine."

A man rips the dress from the woman, but he is too late. Either she has fainted, or she has expired. Passengers from every wagon rush inward with pails of water and thick blankets.

I run back to our wagon and return with an empty flour sack. Just as we manage to slap down a fire along one path, sparks light up in another direction. After an hour, when the scorched ground at our feet seems void of fire, I look around and am amazed to see so many people that I still don't know after a week of traveling together. Our fellow travelers look exhausted, bewildered, and stunned as they realize that the battle is over. We have extinguished the fire that threatened us all.

A man lifts the body of the charred woman from the ground and carries her back toward their wagon. Larkin appears at my side. "Poor woman." He wraps his arm around my waist and walks me back to our wagon.

The boys and men pick up their plates and return to eating, not caring that their beans have gone cold. I dump my plate back into the pot. I can't manage a bite.

An hour later, we stand in the darkness beside a deep grave. I'm glad our men have taken turns and dug deep to ensure that the poor woman's body will not be disturbed. I watch a young man staring blankly as his wife's dead body is lowered into the ground without a coffin. The man holds a small boy named Teddy in his arms. I hope that the boy doesn't understand what is happening.

Captain Meadows delivers a long sermon on the dark, windy prairie. I wish that I had gotten the chance to meet Bridget Sawyer. As the Reverend delivers her eulogy and consoles her widower, Clarkson Sawyer, and her father, Sullivan Pierce, I wish I could offer some sort of comfort. I had naïvely hoped we would avoid tragedy all the way to Oregon, yet here we are, just one week down the trail, burying what I pray will be our only casualty.

Larkin complains about pitching the tent in the dark when we return to camp. "Why didn't we take care of this before supper?" Then Larkin tells Andrew and Christopher to fetch the wagon jack.

I protest. "Larkin, tomorrow is a day of rest. Surely, the boys can grease the axles tomorrow. Everyone is weary tonight."

Larkin argues briefly, then gives in. Just as he's about to crawl into the tent, Agapito approaches. "You're up first tonight, Larkin."

My heart sinks. Larkin looks like he's marching forward to face an executioner as he heads out to take his turn at watch over the stock.

After settling the girls down in the wagon, I spend a few minutes in the tent with the boys. It doesn't take the children long to fall asleep. Though exhausted, I wander into the wagon master's camp, just beyond our tent.

Except for one of the scouts, everyone is gone. He is the man that brought us venison. When he sets down a hairbrush, I realize I've never seen his hair free of the long fat braid he keeps pulled forward over his chest and torso. Though Boss Wheel instructed us not to speak to him or his scouts, I say, "Good evening. I am Dorcas. What is your name?"

I am surprised at how good his English is. "It is nice to meet you. I am Arikta. That means Eagle, ma'am." I watch the graceful movement of his hands as he talks. "Do you need something? I can find Agapito."

"No, I don't need anything. I just wanted to say hello. I like your name. Arikta. It sounds strong and dignified."

He looks pleased to hear a compliment and thanks me. Then he corrects my pronunciation, but it doesn't sound different to my ear than what I said. "uh-RICK-tuh."

I ask what he does with his hands while he talks. He says, "It is called 'hand talk,' and is used to communicate on the plains. It is useful when you need to talk to people who speak different languages."

"Can you teach me?" Sometimes, I'm surprised at the words that escape my lips before I think about what I'm going to say, but I think it would be fun to learn, and I'd also love to have the children learn hand talk.

He looks at me curiously. "None of the wagon women have ever asked this before."

I can't help but laugh. "Everyone is always telling me that I am not like other women. It used to make me sad, but now I am glad. I don't want to be like other women anyway. So, will you teach me, Arikta?"

He doesn't correct the pronunciation of his name this time, and I hope that I'm saying it correctly. "Why not. You learn a little at a time, yes?" I can't help but notice that the way he talks sounds like Agapito. He looks at his fingers as he brings his hands together and overlaps them so that the digits of one hand alternate with the other. He looks up at me and says, "Home."

I copy his sign, and from above, it looks like I have formed a dome-shaped roof with my fingers. I say, "Home," and smile at the Indian boy with serious eyes that remind me of my Andrew.

"Teach me another sign, Arikta."

He holds up his right hand, with his middle finger and index finger pressed together. His other two fingers are closed onto his palm, and his thumb covers his ring finger. He says, "Friend. *Amigo. Ami.*" Perhaps he adds the French word to the English and Spanish because Boss Wheel is half French Canadian.

I make the sign and repeat his words. Then I say, "You and me. We are friends now. Thank you for teaching me, Arikta. If you don't mind me asking, how did you come to be a scout with Boss Wheel and Agapito?"

He turns away briefly, and I wonder whether my question has touched a nerve. He turns back toward me, tucks his hair behind his ears, and gestures, inviting me to sit down. Arikta sits nearby. "I am Pawnee. An orphan. Everyone in my home was killed while I was away hunting. That was four years ago. Agapito found me. He said that he had lost his people too and that we should ride together. He taught me English and some *Español*. Soon we met Boss Wheel and we've been with him ever since."

"I see. Agapito is a good friend, yes?" I resist the urge to laugh. Now, I'm beginning to talk like Agapito also.

Arikta looks down at his feet. I wonder if he's thinking about his Pawnee family. "Agapito is like a father or big brother to me. I would give my life for him, if he asked me to."

I'm astonished at the intensity of the young man's emotions and still can't believe how good his English is. It is even better than Agapito's English. "Can you read books, Arikta?"

"Yes. Agapito taught me how to read and how to write letters. Whenever I find a book, I carry it with me, and read it when I have time. I must travel light, so I only carry one book at a time."

"You are very smart, Arikta. I am impressed."

"Yes, ma'am. Thank you for saying so."

"Please call me Dorcas, not ma'am, since we are friends now."

Nearby, a black and white paint horse stomps his foot. I ask, "Is that your horse, Arikta? That's a good-looking animal."

"Yes," tentatively, he adds, "Dorcas. He is a good friend and very trustworthy."

A wolf howls, and I can't help but cringe. Arikta's horse throws his ears back. Then the horse alternates flopping his ears forward and back as if listening for danger.

Arikta says, "You don't like wolves, do you, Dorcas?"

I make a face. "Never did. Don't know why."

"My horse does not like them either. I call him Howl. He does a good job of warning me when he thinks we are in danger."

Howl stomps his foot again, twice this time, and Arikta stands quickly. I hear footsteps and stand up also. Boss Wheel enters the campsite, grumbling, looks at me, and says, "What do you want?"

I turn away and say, "I was just leaving." I walk toward our wagon and stop briefly, listening from the darkness beyond the wagon master's fire circle.

Boss Wheel asks Arikta gruffly, "What did she want?"

"She did not say."

"Ridiculous women. I wish they would just mind their own business."

I look back over my shoulder. Boss Wheel lies down under the wagon. Arikta takes out a book and holds the pages toward the fire to see them.

I'm exhausted from lack of sleep last night and hope for a good night's sleep tonight. I lean back and find my usual place between sacks of cornmeal, and the fiery image of Bridget Sawyer blazes across the inside of my eyelids.

Instead, I try to force that from my mind. I think about Agapito's kindness, taking in the Pawnee boy, and teaching him so many useful things. What a man, that Agapito Huerta Delgado. I really shouldn't spend so much time thinking about him.

Sunday, April 21

The bonnet above me is brightly lit rather than dark. I sit forward quickly. Did I miss the loud trumpet blasts this morning? I melt back against the bags of meal, recalling that today is Sunday. Our hard-earned day of rest has finally arrived.

Dahlia Jane sits, playing quietly by herself. I'm fortunate that this child is so good at entertaining herself. I glance about and don't see Rose.

I exhale, wondering what today will bring. My back muscles stretch when I sit forward and my hands reach for my chocolate-brown apron. I peek through the opening at the back of the wagon, and my heart sinks at the sight of rain, yet again, and I become aware of the sound of raindrops falling on the wagon cover.

Despite the weather, I'm amazed to see a fire. Andrew watches me climb down from the back of the wagon and smiles. He has constructed a cover for the fire with a slanting roof and has managed to get a good blaze going.

My words of praise flow quickly. "Good thinking. I don't expect I could have managed to light a fire in the rain today without you, Andrew." He seems pleased with himself. I look around us and ask, "Where's your sister?"

Andrew holds both arms wide, palms up. I wonder what is the proper hand sign for, "I don't know?"

I put the rubber rain gear on, set out searching for Rose, and gather firewood as I go along. Fifteen minutes later, I find her hugging the ground beside Bridget Sawyer's grave, overlooking the Kaw River.

"Rose! Child, what's gotten into you?" She barely stirs. Her skin is pale, and her lips look almost blue, instead of red. I drop the firewood I had collected, scoop her skinny body into my arms, and run back toward our wagon. At least she had the sense to put on rain gear.

As I shove her into the back of the wagon, she begins to protest.

"Take off that raincoat and get in under the blankets. I'll get you a hot meal."

"I'm fine, Mama." The way she says those three simple words suggests that I'm overreacting.

"Aren't you cold, Rose?"

"A little bit, I guess. What's the big deal?"

"I can't help it. When I don't know where you are, I worry. Then when I found you, you looked so cold. I thought you were freezing to death."

"If I were cold, I would have come back, Mama."

"Alright, dear." As I walk back to the fire, I'm not so sure. A child her age should have much more sense than she does. I shiver, not from the cold but from fear. It wouldn't surprise me to find Rose frozen on the prairie.

Larkin crawls out of the tent, growling like a bear waking from his long winter nap. I'm glad that he could sleep late after standing watch last night. Then I remember Christopher. Alarmed again, I say, "Where's Christopher? Is he still asleep?"

Andrew says, "Don't worry, Mama. He's over there." Andrew points directly across the ring of wagons. "He went to visit Alvah and Honey."

Larkin stumbles forward, kisses me, and says, "Good morning, Dorcas. You mustn't worry about the children so much. They aren't babies anymore, you know."

"But Larkin, this is wild country. None of us are accustomed to it. We don't know the dangers out here. Besides, I can't help myself. Sometimes, it seems nobody has any sense around here. For heaven's sake, Larkin, put on your raincoat."

"Woman, I'm not a child either."

"I should think not." I turn back toward the river to get the firewood that I abandoned.

When I return, I get provisions from the wagon to make a big pot of porridge and ask Andrew if he could milk Ridge. "Already did, Mama," he says.

I turn toward him, pull him toward me, and hug him tightly. "You're such a good boy, Andrew. How about water?"

"There's a fresh bucketful by the fire."

"Rain or not, I need to do wash today."

Raised voices from the wagon master's camp catch my attention, and I shuffle nearer to see if I can hear what causes the men to disagree. Captain Meadows argues with Boss Wheel, who wants to cross the river this afternoon. Captain Meadows prefers to wait until morning. "Sunday is a day of rest, Mr. Roulette."

"You can rest *after* you cross the river. Or before. Both even. But we *will* cross the river today."

"But it is raining today. Wouldn't it be easier to cross tomorrow?"

"Maybe, but it will be harder to cross if it rains all day and all night. We might be stuck here on the wrong side of the river for days. We agreed that we would have a day of rest on Sunday, whenever possible, but it is up to the wagon master, not the captain, to decide. Besides, the ferry is not busy now. We cross today."

I don't need to listen any longer to know which man will get his way.

Ten minutes later, Agapito rides into camp with Arikta beside him. I make the hand sign for "friend," and Arikta returns the signal. Agapito looks from Arikta back to me and raises an eyebrow. He says, "This afternoon, we cross the river after dinner. Be ready to roll at one, yes?" Before I can respond, the golden mare and the black and white paint carry them to Stillman and Carter's wagon.

The rain picks up and pelts my back as I scrub our soiled clothing. I don't know if it will be possible to remove all of the sweat, dirt, dust, and mud from my dress today, but it is bound to be cleaner than it is now. I hang our dripping garments along a rope tied along the ribs that hold the bonnet over our wagon.

Thanks to Andrew's fire shelter, I have a productive morning despite the cold rain and brutal wind. In addition to laundering our clothing, I've also put up enough biscuits to get us halfway through the coming week.

After dinner, we are ready to roll, as instructed. With our wagon ready, and the children eager, I say to Larkin, "I should check on our neighbors."

"No. They will have to make do on their own. We need to take care of *our* family, Dorcas. Not everybody else's."

"But Jennie is weak. You saw what happened to Bess and Joe at the last crossing. And Addie is afraid of rivers."

"Let the ferrymen and guides do their job, Dorcas."

"But we must help each other, look out for one another. That river is four-hundred feet wide."

"What if something bad happens to our family while you are helping somebody else? Would you be able to forgive yourself?"

"But Larkin, our wagon is too heavy. I'm not a tiny woman, you know. They keep saying we need to lighten the load. I'm worried about the extra weight we are carrying."

Larkin doesn't answer. He looks off to the south, and I can't see his face. Finally, I say. "I'll ride Blizzard across, and lead Ridge as well."

Several wagons have made their way safely across when our turn comes. I stand to the left of the ferry, which is like a large pallet balanced on what looks like canoes. As we're about to enter the river, Agapito shouts from across the river. "Get on the other side, Dorcas." I guess he worries that if I fall off, I could get swept by the current into our wagon, but I'm not worried about falling off or getting thrown. Even so, I move to the other side, as Agapito said to do.

As before, we enter with the current, headed slightly toward the east. Then, we turn within the river toward the crossing on the other side. There are flattened islands in the river. Perhaps they're more like sandbars or mud bars, even.

I'm glad the oxen don't have to pull the wagon through this muddy river, but I worry as I watch the heavily laden ferry. Hornets tumble in my belly as I watch water slightly submerge a corner of the ferry. What will happen when Boss Wheel discovers that we carry hundreds of pounds of extra weight? I don't know how heavy the safe and cookstove are, perhaps seven hundred pounds between them.

Agapito hollers to the ferrymen from the riverbank. "Watch out for the corner," as the ferry begins to tip. The men run to the opposite edge, just in time to prevent a disaster.

I wonder how many more such crossings we must face. I'm sure we will not always be blessed with ferrymen to guide us across, or water that moves as sluggishly as we find in the Kaw River.

I watch the oxen slowly climb the bank when the ferry reaches the opposite shore. They bellow their complaints. Agapito rides forward and says, "Those are good oxen. Three teams should easily pull that load. What have you got in that wagon, Larkin?"

Larkin shrugs. Lamely, he says, "Maybe they're just tired today."

Agapito frowns, rubs his chin, and watches as Larkin drives the wagon out of the way so that the wagons that follow can climb from the river. The wagons that crossed before us have begun to form a circle, and we follow them in formation.

When the teams halt, Larkin whispers loudly to me through his teeth. "Don't tell that bossy Mexican about the safe, y'hear?"

An idea comes to me. "What if we move the safe, or maybe my cookstove to Stillman and Carter's wagon?"

Larkin looks like a weight has lifted from his shoulders. "That's brilliant, Dorcas. See if they can take the stove. I will not part with my safe."

When the boys are safely in place behind us, I approach them. In addition to taking the cookstove, they offer to take some of the provisions. They don't have many belongings between them, and their oxen have had a much easier time.

Before the last wagons clear the river, we've rearranged the wagon's contents. Stillman and Carter have plenty of room, even after adding to their load.

When I return to our wagon, I help Larkin unharness our teams. I can't help saying, "See, Larkin, friends help each other out. Stillman and Carter could have told us that the extra weight was our problem, but instead, they agreed to help us, without argument or complaint."

Larkin is quiet for a while. He must be biting his tongue. I'm sure he wants to say something else, but instead, he says, "We must be sure to thank them."

Mercifully, the weather clears after moving our camp across the river. It's still chilly, but other than that, it's almost pleasant.

After supper, Boss Wheel rides away from camp. Agapito and Arikta relax beside their fire as I approach with Andrew beside me. "Do you gentlemen mind if we visit for a few minutes?"

Agapito rises, doffs his wide-brimmed hat, and invites us to sit. As if just remembering his manners, Arikta quickly stands as well.

I turn to face the scout. "I thought we might learn a few new words, and perhaps Andrew can make some notes for the newspaper. How do you make the sign for *river*?"

Arikta answers, "Take your right hand. Point your finger straight ahead, with your closed fingers facing your body, and pull straight back. River. *Rio. Riviere.*"

Andrew pipes in, "How about horse?"

Arikta says, "Hold your left hand still, keep your fingers pressed together, like the back of a horse. Place your right hand above, divide your pointer finger from the rest of your fingers, and drape the pointer finger over like a rider's leg. Your other three fingers represent the rider's other leg. Drape your right thumb over the base of the left thumb. Horse. *Caballo. Cheval.*"

Andrew and I attempt to follow Arikta's instructions and copy his sign. This one is complicated. Andrew understands immediately, but my clumsy fingers don't seem to find the correct position. Agapito steps forward. He takes my hands in his, and his long, slender fingers rearrange my digits until I'm making the sign perfectly.

I'm so surprised to be touched that I find myself short of breath. I gasp, my hands freeze in place, and words squeak from my throat. "Thank you." I try to take a deep breath and look away from Agapito, who stands close enough to me that I can smell citrus again. I look at Arikta and say, "I like how you say the word in English, Spanish, and French when you make the sign." And then, overcome with curiosity, I can't help but ask, "Agapito, do you wear cologne?"

I feel my face flush with embarrassment, having asked such a personal question.

"No, Dorcas. But I add a few drops of lemon extract to my wash water. It is a small luxury that I allow myself. I love lemons, you see."

"Pardon me for asking. I shall have to make lemon scones for you. You will love them."

Agapito smiles and an eye twitches. Did he just wink at me?

As the day ends, I'm glad that the river crossing was uneventful, but I can't shake the image of Agapito's hands on mine.

Monday, April 22

As I step from the wagon, the cold air hits my face just as the trumpet sound blasts my ears. Though I'm awake before Reveille, the sound still sends me into the air.

Even after hours of slumber, I'm thinking about scones. There isn't time to make them this morning. Perhaps when we stop for the evening.

Our wagon rolls more easily now that the load is lighter. I hope our oxen will not be as weary this week as they were at the end of last week. Although I appreciated a day of rest, I'm sure our animals needed a day to catch up on grazing, even though the grass isn't very high yet.

Our path takes us west and a little bit north. To the south of us, the Kaw River grows farther and farther away, with every step. Andrew walks beside the oxen, Larkin and Christopher walk beside the wagon, and I walk behind. Rose kneels in the back of the wagon, looking off into the distance, where we crossed the river.

I ask, "What are you looking at, dear?"

She says, "That poor woman whose dress caught fire in the rain. She is sad because her family is riding away and leaving her all alone."

I'm a little put off by how Rose claims to be speaking for the dead woman as if she knows her thoughts——as if a dead woman could have thoughts. I sympathize, "I'm sure that her family is sad to leave her here. I feel sorry for her young husband, their small boy, and the poor girl's father, marching off without her." Clarkson Sawyer drives wagon number 8 and is in the lead-off position today, followed by his father-in-law, Sully Pierce.

Finally, Rose abandons her watch and curls up in a ball in the back of the wagon. I lift Dahlia Jane from the wagon, and join Larkin and Christopher. We walk in silence for an hour before Dahlia Jane begins to complain. I reach to pick her up, and Larkin says, "Let the child walk, Dorcas."

After a couple of minutes of listening to the child whine, I've had enough. "If you want to listen to her complain, I'll go somewhere else, but I'm happy to carry her for a while."

"She needs to use her legs. Four is old enough to spend some of the day walking. She can't sit all day like a baby bird in a nest."

"Very well," I say. I increase my pace and walk forward, passing seven wagons until I reach the front of the parade.

A team of mules draws Clarkson's wagon, and he rides on a bench, inside. I can barely see the boy who rides beside him. I raise my voice and say, "Hi, Mr. Sawyer. My name is Dorcas Moon. I want to offer my condolences."

Clarkson replies, "Much obliged," and tips his hat. He doesn't turn his head to look at me, and his face does not express emotion.

"If there's anything I can do, please let us know. We're in wagon number sixteen, eight wagons back. Perhaps you'd like to come to supper. Can you cook, Mr. Sawyer?"

"Thank you, ma'am. I do alright. G'day, ma'am."

The young man doesn't feel like talking, so it would seem. Having been dismissed, I wish him well and wander back to Mr. Pierce's wagon. I try to convey my sympathy to the older man, and he doesn't seem any more communicative than his son-in-law.

Larkin's words ring in my ear. He's always telling me to leave people alone and mind my own business. Sometimes it is hard for me to understand that some people prefer solitude during times of mourning. Perhaps, I would, myself, if I were forced to face such a loss.

When we circle up, late in the afternoon, we hear a crunching sound. People rush toward two wagons that have collided, and I run toward the crash scene as fast as possible.

Agapito directs an oxen-driven wagon into place. The back end is damaged but looks fixable. Then Agapito helps guide the next team into place. A curly, blond-haired man with a southern accent apologizes profusely for losing control of his mules, and his wife clutches two young children to her sides.

The scouts untangle the chains and harnesses while Agapito checks the lead mules' legs for injuries. The mules bray when he touches them, and the scouts unharness the teams. Agapito says, "Give the lead team a couple of days off, Mr. Grimes. I'm sure they'll be fine. You can get by with two teams instead of three along this stretch of the trail."

Boss Wheel stands a short distance from me. He grumbles, cusses under his breath, and mutters, "Greenhorns have no business out here."

The teenage boy from the wagon ahead approaches, followed by two older women. Breathlessly, he says, "Mr. Grimes, is everyone alright? Is there anything I can do to help?"

Mr. Grimes says, "Yes," and looks up at his wife and children in the wagon. "We're fine, but I'm afraid your wagon is damaged, Garland."

The older women look at the wagon, gasp in unison and look at each other. Agapito tells the boy not to worry and assures the women that somebody can fix it. “Don’t worry, Miss Hannah, Miss Miranda, I’m sure we’ll have your wagon repaired before nightfall.”

Stillman Southmaid must have followed me when I ran toward the crash. I didn’t realize that he was standing behind me until he speaks. “I’ve helped build wagons, and I’d be happy to fix your wagon for you.”

Another man steps forward and says, “My name is Schuyler Steele, I’m a wheelwright, and I’d like to help.” I recall Stillman's sore behind complaint. This man is also the beekeeper, whose swarm has sunk stingers into several unhappy neighbors. Young Mr. Steele is among the wagon trains most eligible bachelors, and a wagon full of German sisters compete to catch his eye.

Agapito tells everyone to return to their wagons and tend to their chores. Stillman and Schuyler shake each others’ hands and get to work, looking at how to help Garland and his great aunts. I watch for a minute as they begin to unload the contents of Garland, Hannah, and Miranda Knox’s wagon. Some boxes have fallen over inside, and jewelry has spilled all about.

Hannah gasps. “Oh, look, what a mess? My dear!”

Next to me, a man steps forward. “I’m Leon Humphries, ma’am. Would you like me to help you set things straight?”

Instead, Miranda answers. “We’d be much obliged, Mr. Humphries.”

Back at our wagon, Larkin has built a fire, and I prepare supper. Fresh meat would be most welcome, but we’ll have to settle for bacon and beans for dinner again tonight. As they warm at the edge of the fire, I combine flour, oats, sugar, saleratus, butter, goat’s milk, a generous amount of lemon extract, and one of our precious few eggs. Then, I stir the dry batter and press it into the Dutch oven. I dish up beans and bacon for Larkin and the children, and afterwards, I prepare a curd from butter, sugar, lemon extract, and three more eggs. I wish we had brought more than one laying hen, and that Gloria could be counted on to lay an egg every day, but she's not that reliable along the trail, not that I can blame the poor creature.

I cringe as I imagine Larkin chastising me for using a week's worth of eggs to make scones, just to give away. Maybe he will not say anything. When the scones finish cooking, I cut them into small pieces and serve Larkin and the children first. I put the remaining scones into a small basket and head back to the Grimes and Knox wagons.

Stillman and Schuyler are just finishing with their repairs. Miranda thanks them as Hannah glares at the Grimes family. I have just enough scones for everyone. Butler Grimes, his wife Betty, and their children, Dean and Lulu, seem very friendly, and I like listening to their southern accents. Agapito watches from a short distance away, prepared to help if needed. I bring the last scone to him, and offer him some curd to smear on top of it. "They're lemon," I say, smiling at him.

The corners of his mouth curl into a smile, and I can feel my heartbeat quicken. It strikes my mind that I'd like to take my index finger and touch that dimpled spot at the corner of his mouth. I tell him that I've got the coffeepot on the fire if he wants to stop by when he's done.

I ask if anybody else would like curd. There's barely enough to go around, and I wish I could have made more. I hurry back to our wagon and say, "It looks like the Knox's wagon is all fixed up, just like new."

Larkin looks up at me and says, "Who cares? So what? What does that have to do with us?"

I gasp. "Larkin. Stop that. You know better than that. What's gotten into you?"

"It's all we can do to worry about ourselves, Dorcas. We can't get caught up in every little thing that happens to people on this wagon train. I never even heard of the Knox or Grimes families until today."

"Just because you haven't met them, that doesn't mean that we shouldn't help them. That's not how we were raised, Larkin. That's not how we are. What if we needed help? I bet they would help us. That's what civilized people do."

"Civilized? In case you hadn't noticed, we're not a part of civilization anymore. This is Indian country."

"Indian country? Indian country!" I can't help but stomp my feet in anger. "What does that have to do with anything? I swear!" I grab our bucket and walk down to Cross Creek.

I feel like steam puffs from my ears, and then the irony of the creek's name tickles my fancy. I relax and start to giggle. Then I notice that I'm not alone. The taller scout stands motionless next to his horse beside the waterway, watching me from the corner of his eyes. Perhaps he was hoping that I wouldn't notice him if he didn't move.

"I don't think we've met or been properly introduced. My name is Dorcas Moon. Do you speak English?"

He taps his chest with his palm and says his name, "Dembi Koofai. Means stone face." Then he points to his black Appaloosa and says, "Horse. Coffeepot."

I've never seen a prettier steed. The front half is dark-colored, his muzzle is more brown than black, and his rump is bright white with small black spots. I look back at the young man and ask him how old he is.

He turns ever so slightly toward me, holds up both hands, closes his fists, and then opens them again.

I say, "Twenty? You are 20-years-old?"

He nods once and becomes silent and motionless again.

I deduce that the young man with the long straight hair is friendly, but shy. Something about the look in his eyes makes me think that he has suffered a lot, and trusts little. Tentatively, I say, "May I ask about your people?" I hold up my hand and look at my fingers to make sure I'm correctly making the sign for 'friend.'

He answers, "Shoshone. Mountain people. West." The English he knows conveys meaning, perhaps like hand signals, but doesn't convey emotions or include connecting words. His head tips back proudly, ever so slightly, and I can tell he is watching me, despite standing mostly perpendicular to me. He is a striking young man with smooth, dark skin, high, prominent cheekbones, and smoldering eyes.

I say, "It is a pleasure to meet you. I hope that we will become good friends. Good night, Dembi Koofai."

The pail of water spills over its edge as I climb up the banks of Cross Creek and return to camp. I pour the bucket into the barrel that rests on a small shelf attached to our wagon and replace the round, wooden lid.

Then I climb up into our wagon. Rose and Dahlia are already settled in. I pull my blanket up to my chin, and Larkin's words return to my ear. "Indian country."

Tuesday, April 23

Another rude awakening blasts us from slumber at three, as usual. Andrew sparks a fire before I climb from the wagon. Something about my serious, dark-haired boy makes me want to hug him whenever I see him. I'm sure it will not be long until he pushes me away, as his sister does.

I ask, "What will we have for weather today?"

"Sunny and hot. Mark my words, Mama." I think about Fritz Franzwa's fancy weather gadgets and wonder whether he would predict the same.

I add wood to Andrew's fire while he retrieves the post from The Hub. What events will be newsworthy today?

As the morning wears on, it gets warmer and warmer. The sun shines brightly, just as Andrew predicted. I'm not sure how he does it. He says that he's merely lucky. He thinks for a moment, and the day's weather just comes to him. I can't remember when he has ever been wrong, when he chances to make a prediction. It is by far our warmest travel day yet. I venture to guess that temperatures are well above seventy degrees.

Christopher asks if he can walk with Alvah Nye for a while. Andrew says, "Yes. I'll walk with the oxen. Go on back and walk with Alvah, if you'd like."

I look at Andrew and smile. I say, "Maybe he was asking for his Mama's permission."

"I'm sorry, Mama. I wasn't thinking. It's alright, isn't it?"

I laugh. "Of course, sure it is. I was just teasing you." I walk quietly beside him for a while. I hardly cringe when he cracks the whip above the oxen now. Still, I'm glad that Andrew usually just taps their rumps with the tip of the whip. "Isn't it surprising how quickly we've grown used to marching across the prairie?"

He smiles back at me. "Yes. I like it. You never know what will happen next."

"That's for sure." I repeat his words back to him. "You *just* never know what is going to happen next."

Suddenly, a large snake, thick as my arm, appears in the grass to my left. It coils into a pile, raises its tail, and shakes its rattle. I jump back. It uncoils and slithers back into the grass, away from us. My heart roars in my chest, and I'm not even that afraid of snakes, but I've never heard a snake rattle at me before.

Calmly, Andrew says, "It's probably the heat that brings them out. You'd better be on the lookout. We'll probably see a lot of snakes."

"Perhaps you should write about snakes in the newspaper today, Andrew. Maybe the wagon masters can tell you what people need to know about them."

Andrew likes the idea. He almost always approves of my suggestions, whereas Larkin usually wants to bicker, and Rose wants to ignore whatever I say. Christopher defers to his brother and sister, instead of me, sometimes. I shake my head and smile. Thank goodness for Andrew.

My prideful, motherly moment comes to a quick end as I hear a deafening scream ahead of us. My skin prickles when a woman runs toward us, screeching like demons are chasing her. It takes me a minute to realize that she is the doctor's wife, Charlotte Appleyard.

I block her path, and she crashes into me. I wrap my arms around the woman. "Charlotte! Mrs. Appleyard! What's wrong?"

She backs away from me and grabs her head like she has a pounding headache. "Snake. Snakes!" She hops about the prairie in front of me as if snakes are writhing about her ankles. "Help me, Dorcas. It was horrible. It shook its rattling tail at me, opened its mouth, showed me its fangs, and stuck its hideous tongue out at me. It gave me the evil eye, and then it struck at me." She turns around and points back toward her place in line. The Appleyard wagon is number fourteen, immediately beyond the wagon master's.

I try to reassure Charlotte, and she asks if she can walk with us for a while. "You are so comforting and understanding. I'm afraid Hollis would just laugh at me."

I shake my head, jokingly. "Men! Insensitive brutes."

Charlotte looks at me, nods her head, and says, "Don't I know it? Even the good ones, like Hollis, sometimes just can't help themselves. I hope I never see another monster like that again, long as I live."

Hoping to distract her, I suggest that Andrew interview Charlotte. I'd like to get to know her better myself. Aside from her fear of snakes, she seems like a very rational woman, sensible as it is to have a healthy respect for rattlesnakes.

She seems to enjoy talking to my journalist. "I must confess, I'm homesick, Andrew. I don't know why we decided to leave our home in Richmond. One afternoon, Hollis suggested we move to Oregon. I was surprised that Violet and Martin were excited to go. It was like they conspired against me. What I wouldn't do to be sitting in the parlor, having a cup of tea this afternoon instead of walking endlessly across the prairie? From now on, as long as we're in snake country, I'm going to ride in the wagon."

We take turns asking Charlotte questions, and we're surprised to learn that she helps her husband when he needs a nurse, and she also enjoys making salves. She talks about herbs, their healing qualities, and collecting plants whenever she sees ones with special powers.

After a while, Charlotte's seventeen-year-old daughter, Violet, approaches, looking for her mother. Charlotte says, "Violet, we're being interviewed for the newspaper. This young man, Andrew, wants to know what scares *you*."

Violet curls her upper lip. "I'm afraid of heights. I don't like the idea of falling. When our wagon goes downhill, my stomach turns. Whenever I see a hill coming, I beg Father to stop. I'd jump from the wagon while it rolls, but jumping is just like falling. Nope, I don't like it at all. Could we talk about something else?"

The girl looks up into my face and says, "Oh dear, Mrs. Moon. You don't look too good."

I'm stunned by the young lady's rudeness.

Violet continues, "I think you have a sunburn."

I realize that my head isn't covered. Of all days, I have to forget *today*. I thank her for telling me and excuse myself. "I'll be right back. I had better get my bonnet before it gets any worse."

When I return, Charlotte says, "We'd better get back before Hollis sends Martin after me, too."

After they're gone, I mention to Andrew, "It's nice to meet new friends. It's too bad about snakes and sunburns, though. What else will we encounter on this grand adventure?"

Andrew snaps the whip, and I jump. "I'm sorry, Mama. I should have noticed that you weren't wearing your bonnet. I'll try to keep my eye on you in the future."

I gingerly touch my cheeks. I hadn't noticed until Violet mentioned it, but my skin feels tight. My head begins to ache, and my tongue is dry. "I'm going to get some water, Andrew. Do you want any?"

"Sure, Mama."

While the wagon rolls, I scoop water from the barrel with the tin dipper and take a deep drink. I splash warm water on my face, and jog to catch back up to the barrel as the wagon continues forth. I fill the dipper again, catch up to Andrew, and trade the water for the bullwhip.

Soon, I'm alone beside the oxen. Larkin, Rose, and Dahlia Jane plod along a short distance away. I look back, and Andrew runs to catch up, having hung the dipper back on its peg beside the water barrel. When he reappears beside me, Andrew says, "If I knew Christopher would be gone all day, I might not have let him go."

"He sure enjoys spending time with Alvah, doesn't he?"

"Yes, Mama. Christopher wants to be a hunter, just like Alvah Nye. And he wants a dog, too."

I feel my breath catch in my windpipe. Honey is a good dog, and I'm beginning to trust her a little bit, always careful to watch her mouth when I pat her on the head. I don't mind letting Dahlia Jane have a kitten someday, but I hope to avoid having a dog in the house.

When the long, hot day ends and the wagons circle, Christopher runs across the ring, shouting. I look at him as he approaches, and struggle to see what he has. Something swings from each hand, and as he gets closer, I realize he's carrying dead snakes.

"Mama, Mama! Alvah says these make great stew. We have meat for dinner."

I'm horrified. Christopher has three snakes in each hand. Every one of them is longer than he is tall. Proudly, he says, "I killed this one. I found its hole, poked a stick in it, and when the snake stuck his head out, I whacked it off with Alvah's machete. Isn't it a beast, Mama?"

I stutter for lack of words and say, "Don't you know that rattlesnakes are poisonous? If a snake bites you, it could kill you."

"I know. That's what Alvah said. He told me that I shouldn't have done it without permission. But it was so exciting." My nine-year-old is the most adventurous of my children, and reminds me of myself at his age.

Christopher hands me the snakes, but I back away. "I'm not touching them, Christopher. Take them to the wagon master."

"Sure thing, Mama." I gasp and remind myself that I fear wolves, not snakes.

Half an hour later, Christopher returns with a pail full of skinned snake. I glance into the bucket. The peach-colored meat looks less frightening without the diamond-patterned skin attached. Christopher says, "The tall Indian showed me how to skin the snakes."

"I'm glad. Maybe the *tall Indian* can also tell us how to cook them." I take Christopher by the hand, with the bucket of snake meat in my other hand, and approach the wagon master's camp.

I let go of Christopher's hand, set the pail on the ground, and make the friend sign. "Good evening, Dembi Koofai. Could you teach us how to cook rattlesnakes?"

He pats himself on the chest and says, "I cook."

Christopher looks at me and says, "You know him?"

"Yes, Christopher. We introduced ourselves to each other last night. He is a very nice man."

Christopher smiles and says, "Just like Alvah Nye."

I agree. "Yes, just like Alvah."

When the snakes finish cooking, Dembi Koofai hands me a dish with a little bit of stew in it. "Eat."

I force myself to taste it. I'm not sure whether it tastes more like pork or quail, a little gamey, but good. I say, "Do you men mind if we share with everybody?"

Hearing no dissension, I tell Christopher to let everybody know that we've got a big pot of rattlesnake stew at our camp if they'd like to come over for a taste. I figure it is a good way to meet new friends, though I've managed to introduce myself to almost everyone already.

From the shade of our wagon, I watch as Christopher stands triumphantly in front of the fire. As people come and go, he introduces Alvah Nye as our snake slayer. Alvah stands nearby, humbly deflecting attention and warning passengers about the poisonous reptiles.

Larkin grumbles in the shade at my side. "What a long way we've come, Dorcas. Remember when people used to come from far away to dine at Storrs House Inn?" My cakes and pastries were locally famous. Larkin shakes his head and says, "Now, we're serving rattlesnakes to strangers in the middle of nowhere."

Wednesday, April 24

This morning, Agapito blows the trumpet at four instead of three. The wagon masters told us we could expect a lighter day, and if we make good time, the stock will have extra time to graze when we reach Scott Spring.

As I go about my morning chores, I feel like someone is watching me. I check my head and make sure that my bonnet is firmly tied down and that my hair is properly bundled up within it.

The fire crackles, and the coffeepot warms as I think about whether I can serve my family anything different. Then I recall yesterday's rattlesnake stew and decide that plain old hot porridge will be fine this morning.

Then I turn and see Agapito leaning against his wagon, watching me. I glance to my left and check to my right. There's nobody but me here, so he can't be looking at anybody else. I'm uncertain whether fear, or excitement tumbles in my belly as I walk over and wish him a good morning.

He shakes his head from side to side, and says, "I have never met anyone like you, Dorcas. After years of leading people down one trail or another, I've met many people, but you are one-of-a-kind."

I'm sure he's being nice, but I can't help but feel like I've done something wrong. "I'm sorry, Agapito. I'm afraid I don't know what you mean."

"Me neither," he says. "I keep watching you, asking myself what you are going to do or say next. Then you come up with something I never thought of, or expected. Even Dembi Koofai can not stop talking about you. He hardly ever says anything. I may not know what will happen next, but I sure am glad you signed on with us."

I'm stunned. I don't know what to make of Agapito's revelation. Lamely, I say, "Thank you for the compliment."

I try to turn away, but still feel the heat of his intense gaze. I turn back and say, "Tell me about your life before Boss Wheel and the Oregon Trail——before you met Arikta."

Agapito moistens his lips with his tongue and then looks down at the space between us. "Ten years ago, I married an enchanting girl, my age. We were happy and so in love. Morning, noon, and night, my world revolved around Merced. When she died, I took it hard." Agapito looks up toward the sky. "God blessed us with a daughter, and we named our angel Sarita. I worked the Santa Fe Trail and decided I didn't want to be away from them anymore, so they joined me on my final trip to Santa Fe. We were going to move there. I had saved money for a small rancheria. One day, while I was hunting, outlaws attacked the wagon train. They killed half of the travelers before our hunting party returned and chased them away. Merced clung to life, holding Sarita's lifeless body. Our baby was only four, the same age as Dahlia Jane. Merced told me that she would love me forever, not just this lifetime, and I told her that I would never marry again. With her last breath, Merced told me *not* to keep that promise, but I have."

Emotion overwhelms me, and tears stream down my cheeks. When I sniffle, Agapito looks at me. Then he says, "I have not been back to Santa Fe since."

"That is so sad, Agapito. Thank you for telling me." I grasp his arm, just behind his elbow. "I'm sorry about what happened to your wife and baby.

Merced and Sarita. What beautiful names. If you ever want to talk about them, I'm happy to listen."

"This is the first time I have spoken of them." A tear squeezes from the corner of his eye. "I didn't think I was strong enough to tell anybody. Thank you for listening, Dorcas."

Larkin appears beside me. Agapito turns his head away, and Larkin looks back and forth between us, suspiciously. With a frown, his eyes lock with mine. He sounds agitated when he speaks. "It's almost time to harness the teams. Is breakfast ready?"

I pat Agapito on the forearm and then turn away. Larkin seems surprised when I take his arm for the brief stroll to our campfire. I can't decide if I care whether Larkin thinks something happened that shouldn't have happened. He's silent when we reach our campfire. He pours himself a cup of coffee, and I say, "I'll have breakfast ready in a couple of minutes." He turns away with a brief grunt.

Today I walk beside Christopher. After yesterday, it is his turn to drive the oxen. The weather is cooler, and the snakes are less active. Hour after hour, Christopher talks about his day with Alvah and Honey, and all the snakes that Alvah killed while Christopher drove Alvah's team of oxen.

I should listen more attentively to my son, but my mind wanders hopelessly. I can't stop thinking about Agapito's story, and his promise to Merced.

Why have I allowed myself to dream about Agapito? I'm a happily married woman, a mother of four, yet I always think things I shouldn't, especially about men I could never have, even if I weren't married. Usually, those thoughts go away after a couple of days. Agapito stubbornly remains the object of my desire, regardless of attempts to dispel my longing for him.

We stop for a fast dinner at midday, then walk through the afternoon. Andrew appears at my side. He's breathing fast. I ask, "Have you been running, Andrew?"

"Yes, I have just come from wagon number 28. I met a nice family there. Landon and Cornelia Young are from Falls Village, Connecticut. They have a three-year-old son, Landon Jr., and an Irish Setter named Chestnut." Andrew glances at me, and I guess he sees me flinch when he mentions the dog. "Don't worry, Mama, the dog is very friendly, just like Honey. Anyway, Landon has a sister named Grace in wagon number four. Landon and Grace have another sister named Sarah, who rode with Boss Wheel last year. When outlaws attacked the wagons along the Snake River, Sarah's husband stopped a bullet, and she became a widow. When they reached Oregon, she sent Landon a letter asking him to come along. Sarah and her children are staying with a family they met last year until Landon and Grace can get there. Can you believe it, Mama? I asked if I could print their letter in the newspaper, and Landon said 'yes.' Do you think I should, Mama?"

I don't know what to think about this news. I never realized that wagon trains were in such jeopardy from outlaws along the trail. I scratch my jaw, forgetting my sunburn for a moment, and moan from the pain of my own touch. I say, "I hate to scare everyone unnecessarily."

Andrew says, "But Mama, doesn't everyone have a right to know? Maybe we can be more wary as we travel. Perhaps we should learn more about self-defense."

I glance at Andrew. "I guess. If it is alright with Mr. Young, it isn't up to me whether he shares the letter he got from his sister."

Though we probably don't have much farther to go, I'm not feeling too well. I tell the boys that I must climb into the wagon and rest for a few minutes. Hopefully, the oxen can endure the extra weight.

Thoughts bounce around my crowded head as I stare at the bright bonnet above me. Tools clamor against the wagon sides. The chains that link the oxen to the wagon rattle. The wooden underpinnings groan as the wagon hits pebbles, rocks, and ruts along the path. Braying mules, bellowing oxen, nickering horses, the bleating goat, and the squawking hen all make noises that are plainer to hear when lying alone in the back of a moving wagon. Yet still, the wild howling of wolves in my imagination rises above the din. I think of Dahlia Jane's people with cat faces and imagine a pack of wild outlaws with wolfish faces attacking the wagon train, and ripping everybody apart, limb from limb, just like that poor man we saw, dug from his shallow grave.

My head throbs. Perhaps it comes with sunburns. I thought that this would be a grand adventure, and it is, but I'm not sure whether we can meet its challenges. Are we strong enough?

Somehow, I fall asleep. When the wagon comes to a halt, I sit forward, surprised, as if expecting to hear the fiery trumpet blasts. My face feels sweaty, and I swipe it dry with my sleeve. Then I remember having climbed aboard to rest. We must have reached our encampment for the evening.

I'm not accustomed to napping in the afternoon, and I don't think I like it. I don't feel rejuvenated but climb down nevertheless. The cool breeze feels heavenly. I fill my lungs with fresh air, and then, I tend to the chores.

When our stock is settled, Andrew pulls the pole from the wagon, affixes today's post to the underside of the lid, and carries it to The Hub.

The fire begins burning steadily, and I put water on for rice, fry bacon, and set the coffeepot above the flames. Rose and Dahlia Jane sit in the shade beneath the wagon, resting after a long day's hike, and then, the boys join them.

I'm glad to be feeling better and hopeful that whatever ailed me has passed. Even my sunburned face feels cooler. I unload boxes from the back of the wagon and carry them to the fire's edge. As I finish preparing supper, I notice a crowd beginning to form at The Hub. While unpacking tin plates, cups, and flatware, the old saying about news spreading like wildfire comes to mind. When I call the family to dinner, we sit on our boxes and watch what looks like the entirety of our rolling village, except for us, gathered in animated conversations.

I glance at Andrew, and he rolls his shoulders. A raised voice from the wagon master's camp reaches my ears. "What the dickens is going on with those pilgrims? Something's got them fired up. Go see what's gnawing at 'em, Pito."

I make a face at Andrew, and he shrugs. The boy puts his tin plate on top of the box, and I follow him toward the crowd.

Agapito shouts, "Ladies! Gentlemen. Attention, *por favor*." With conversations settled, he continues, "Good afternoon, everyone. What is on your minds this fine afternoon, eh?"

Our friend, Esther Bump, angrily says, "Is it true, Mr. Pito?"

Samuel Grosvenor shouts, "We'll all be killed." Then he hiccups.

Horace Blocker gripes, "We're just like a bunch of ducks, sitting, waiting to be shot." Then he nervously cracks his knuckles.

Addie Bull complains, "We should have stayed home instead of traipsing across the wilderness. This procession is cursed."

Agapito holds his hands out in front of him. "What are you all talking about?"

A man named Galusha Gains sneers. "The newspaper." He points to the post. "It says that outlaws attacked your train last year and killed a man along the Snake River. How many outlaws were there, Pito? Why, I'll put a bullet in every one of them. Just wait until I draw a bead on 'em. They won't know what hit 'em, by golly. No mercy, I say!" The hunter's lip curls into a sneer.

Landon Young tells Agapito about the letter he got from his sister, Sarah Terwilliger, while Agapito nods in confirmation, finally understanding the situation.

Leon Humphries tips his hat back and says, "I don't know what everybody is so worried about. Those outlaws are probably a million miles away by now, living large." He nods his head vigorously, as if hoping that everyone will agree with him. Why should he care?

Agapito answers, "It is true. Yes. Last year, three or four outlaws attacked the train. We lost one man, Mr. Terwilliger, but we held them off, and they moved on. Sad to say, some people would rather take things that do not belong to them than work to acquire riches themselves, no? Maybe you do not read about it in the newspapers back home, but being attacked by outlaws *is* one of the hazards of traveling The Oregon Trail. We will do everything we can to protect you. This is why we have expert scouts. This is why we teach women to load the guns, eh?"

The grumbling crowd begins to dissipate, returning to their wagons. Perhaps some are reassured, and others have a new worry to trouble them. I bet many of us have a renewed interest in our self-defense.

When Agapito returns to the wagon master's camp, I hear the gruff voice of Boss Wheel. This time, I'm not eavesdropping. He's so loud, I can't help overhearing. Boss Wheel growls, "I should have known that it had something to do with that busybody woman and her family."

Agapito says, "I think they done us a favor, Boss."

Boss Wheel coughs and says, "I wouldn't be so sure about that."

Thursday, April 25

THE FLAPPING CANVAS WAGON cover awakens me before the trumpet. A howling wind reminds me of the rainy, muddy day we had at the beginning of our journey. The scouts circulate as we begin to rise, chanting, "No fires today. Too windy." At least it isn't raining.

A fierce wind smacks me in the face when I hop down from the wagon and threatens to hurl my bonnet across the prairie. I huddle against the wagon's side and tie the strings tightly beneath my chin.

I call to the boys in the tent and pull Christopher through the flaps. I tell Andrew to wait for me to return while I carry his brother to the wagon. When I get back, he says, "Don't worry about me, Mama."

I resist the urge to take his hand and wish that he would let me carry him. He doesn't complain when I follow him, and after he boards, I hand each of the children a biscuit. "I know it's not much of a breakfast. I wish I had something else to give you this morning." I fetch water and hope the wind doesn't blow too much sand into it on my way back. It's bad enough to think of the sand the children will ingest with their biscuits.

Larkin groans when I return to the tent flaps. "What new hell is this?"

I wish I had an answer for him. I reach a hand into the tent and pull him through the opening. He stands, eyes squinting, leaning into the wind, with his hands rubbing the small of his back. I know it pains him, and sleeping on the ground doesn't help. I say, "I'll get the tent, and then I'll help with the teams."

Wrestling sheets on a clothesline is good preparation for taking down a tent during a windstorm. I can't fold it neatly. Instead, I shove it into place in the back of the wagon, glad to be done with the task.

The oxen bellow as we retrieve them. I'm glad I don't have to harness them alone. We've become experts at yoking them, and Larkin is particularly proficient with them. I know his back bothers him, and every time he bends over or lifts something, his face twists in pain. I try to anticipate what he needs next, so I can do the bending, squatting, and lifting. When we finish harnessing the teams, Larkin says, "Thank you, love."

He leans forward, kisses my lips, and I say, "It looks like it is going to be a long day." The ordinary kiss feels like the morning chores rather than an amorous moment. It conveys his appreciation, but doesn't distract me from the harsh reality of the coming miles. I add, "Do you think we can let the children ride in the wagon this morning?"

Larkin frowns. I know it goes against his better judgment. He says, "Why not?" and smacks his hat down on his head to prevent it from blowing away.

We're off again with nine blasts of the trumpet and a crack of the whip. The fierce wind swirls furiously about us. I walk along beside my husband, thinking about our marriage vows. For better or worse, today would seem more like the latter, but there's a certain feeling that goes along with weathering a hardship together. Today, it feels like we are a team, like a fourth pair of oxen, drawing the wagon up the trail.

Our wagon is the seventh in line today. There isn't a good place in line during a gale, but I'm happy we're not farther back. I don't know which wagon brings up the rear, but I'm glad it isn't ours.

An hour along, I tap Larkin's shoulder. I shout at him above the howling winds. "Want a neckerchief?" A gust blows sand into my mouth as I retrieve face coverings. The wagon slows as I climb aboard. I imagine how the oxen must feel and wish that I could cover their faces as well. After helping the children cover their noses and mouths, I stretch a neckerchief onto my own and deliver one to Larkin.

We barely stop to rest at midday. Instead of letting up, the wind only seems to blow harder. Just like breakfast, there's no chance for a warm dinner. Despite the relentless blowing from the northeast, the children walk during the afternoon.

I try to endure harsh conditions without griping and quietly agree when my family complains around me. I hope the wind dies away soon. I'd like nothing more than to sneak down to the river after dark and wash the gritty sand from my scalp. My eyes are dry, and I try to cry so that I can flush dirt away with my tears. Even my ears are full of filth.

By the middle of the afternoon, we reach the Black Vermillion River, which empties into the Big Blue. I'm sure Boss Wheel would like to have us cross this afternoon, but he must know that we don't have it in us to face a river crossing during a windstorm. We unharness the oxen, and lead them to join the gathered herd. Agapito taps Larkin's shoulder. "You're on watch until nine, Larkin." My husband's shoulders sag, and I wish I could take his place as I walk back to the wagon alone. Why does it seem like they call Larkin to watch so frequently? How do they know that each man gets their fair share of service? Perhaps everyone feels like their number comes up too often.

With the back of my hand, I shoo the children into the wagon, and a nursery rhyme comes to mind. It plays like a song in my head, "There was an old woman who lived in a shoe. She had so many children, she didn't know what to do. She gave them some broth without any bread; and whipped them all soundly and put them to bed." I don't have any broth, but I've got bread. I wouldn't whip them, but the wind sure has. I don't know who Mother Goose was, but I can identify with the old woman who lived in a shoe.

I draw the bonnet tightly over the wagon bows and hang a blanket over the round openings, fore and aft. Having battened down the hatches, I wither onto a sack of flour, exhausted. Even the children are worn out, and lay beside me, motionless.

When I awaken, sometime later, the wind seems to have faded, though it hasn't stopped completely. I look at the children and say, "Maybe I can cook supper now."

Rose scoffs, "You were babbling nursery rhymes in your sleep."

Dahlia Jane giggles. Christopher asks if he can go, and Andrew tells me that he will help with chores. It occurs to me that Andrew is becoming jealous of Christopher's time away with Alvah Nye. Rose rolls her eyes and doesn't seem inclined to move from the back of the wagon, where she scribbles notes in her journal.

I gather wood from along the river, and scout out prospects for a bath. When I return to camp, Andrew says that the wagon masters now permit small fires, but warn us to be careful. We gather blackened rocks that look like they have also served other emigrants. I use a shovel to dig a shallow hole and shake dirt from the roots of dried grass. The wind has sucked the moisture from everything, and the tinder in my box lights on the first spark. It's hard not to think of poor Bridget Sawyer whenever I work with fire, and I'm cautious about the hem of my dress whenever I'm beside it.

When supper is ready, I take a big plate of bacon and beans to Larkin, who watches over the oxen and picketed horses. A stray gust of wind stirs a cloud of dust, peppering the top of the meal with an extra, earthly seasoning, and I frown at the thought of it. I see Boss Wheel, sitting on his horse, Clipper, a short distance away. As I walk back to camp, I wonder what Boss Wheel does all the time. He's barely ever present in camp.

While I've got a good fire going, I stir batter for biscuits, having learned how important it is to have a ready supply. While I sit, waiting for my fourth batch of biscuits to finish cooking, something catches my eye, a quarter way around the ring——another fire! I jump from the box I'm sitting on, shouting, "Wagon on fire. Wagon on fire!"

Agapito and Dembi Koofai rush from the wagon master's camp. Agapito shouts, "Grab a blanket. Bring a bucket. A wagon is on fire."

Dry canvas burns fast when the wind blows. An older man stumbles from the back of his flaming wagon. Folks from neighboring wagons descend upon the man's wagon, fecklessly slapping at the bonnet with saddle blankets.

Agapito yells, "Rip the bonnet off." Flaming chunks of canvas blow from the wagon. We run and chase them as they land in the dry grass, stomping them with our boots and smothering them with blankets. The old man's wagon stands naked on the prairie, the uncovered bows bending over the wagon top look like cattle skeletons blanching on the prairie.

Andrew appears beside me. "That's Sullivan Pierce's wagon. He's the father of the woman whose dress caught fire last week."

Nearby, Clarkson Sawyer clutches his son, Teddy, and steps toward his father-in-law. He looks at the wagon, then back at the older man as if he doesn't know what to say.

Agapito speaks. "I can loan you a bonnet, Sully. I carry an extra one in my wagon. You can buy me a new one when we get to Fort Laramie."

Boss Wheel appears beside Agapito, shaking his head and rubbing his chin through his beard's thick, wiry hairs.

Clarkson asks, "What happened?"

Sully looks down at the ground, ashamed. "I struck a friction match and lit a candle so I could find my spectacles. Next thing I know, a gust of wind blows through my wagon and knocks the candle from my hand, and then the cover bursts into flames."

Boss Wheel curses and adds, "Stupid greenhorns. I told you the rules. No fire in the wagons. Idiots." He turns and strides away, cursing in French. He tosses a stiff right leg over his horse and disappears between two wagons.

Compassion for Sully saddens me. Yes, he didn't follow the rules, and he shouldn't have lit that candle, but that doesn't excuse making him feel like a criminal.

I watch Agapito and Dembi Koofai cover Sully's wagon with bright new canvas while Andrew interviews witnesses for *The Rolling Home Times*. Agapito speaks kindly to the older man. Perhaps he's thinking about how the man must feel, having lost his daughter recently. Maybe he is trying to make up for Boss Wheel's harshness. I can't help admiring Agapito's kindness, and try to remember if I've ever seen him angry or irritable. Instead, I recall how outlaws killed his wife and baby girl on the Santa Fe trail.

Andrew touches my arm, and I realize that I have been daydreaming. Sully's new wagon cover stands bright against the darkening sky, and the last of the good Samaritans return to their wagons.

It has grown late, and hopes of bathing have lapsed. With my fingertips, I massage my scalp in an attempt to dislodge stubborn, gritty sand from my head.

Friday, April 26

When the trumpet blasts the moon from the sky, it is all I can do to lift myself from a reclining position.

Yesterday, I thought I was feeling better. I don't remember a sunburn ever making me feel so miserable. My skin feels warm and tight, my sandpaper lips are dry and cracked, and I feel like I haven't bathed in months.

As the day begins, the air is cool but dry, which is a blessing, but all I want to do is return to napping beneath my quilt in the wagon. Larkin and the children shuffle silently as they perform our morning chores, and after nine trumpet blasts signal our departure, I climb back on board.

The ride isn't comfortable, but I prefer solitude when I'm not feeling well. I tell myself that I could walk beside the wagon, if I must. There's a constant, dull ache in my head, and I have no ambition. My limbs feel weighty, and I prefer to have my body pitched about rather than flex my muscles to maintain my usual place in the wagon. I think about our eggs suspended in a barrel of oats, and marvel that they don't break. It's a ridiculous thought, but I wish I were riding in a big grain barrel. No wonder, except for Dahlia Jane, the children don't like to ride in the wagon. Even so, the minutes melt into hours, and the hours float by like clouds in the sky, until the wagons stop for dinner.

As the wagon draws to a halt, I jostle awake and quickly sit forward. I grab my knees protectively. My breath comes fast, and sweat covers my face. The wolf dream has returned, yet again. I rub my eyes and try to shake the trio of canids from my mind, but vividly see the circling beasts, and in the distance, a fourth wolf watches his brothers.

I run my fingers through my hair in a quick search for tangles, don my bonnet, and join my family for our mid-day meal. The cool morning has given way to a hot day, and I wonder if the mercury touches eighty degrees yet. I drive the oxen throughout the afternoon, feeling better, not one hundred percent, but I certainly can't sleep anymore.

It's still hot when the wagons circle for the night. I'm encouraged by a lovely-looking site. Lush, verdant forests and meadows surround us. Spring flowers dot the grassy fields like my floral dress, except the varied blossoms represent all the colors of the rainbow, rather than just pink and white. The long-anticipated Alcove Springs campground exceeds expectations.

A lovely spring sprays water over a rock ledge just beyond the circled wagons. Beneath a ten-foot waterfall, we find a shielded place to bathe. Our men have been banished as women take turns splashing and scrubbing in the frigid water after a hot day along the trail.

After dinner, I sit beside the fire, brushing my hair. My tingly skin feels refreshed. The cold, invigorating water has done wonders. The absence of dirt from my scalp feels wonderful, and I begin to hum. My blissful moment is interrupted by a buzz in my ear. After a moment of quiet, I feel a mosquito's stinger pierce my neck. I slap my skin and brush the insect away, set my brush down, and stand up beside the fire. Another bug lands on my forehead, and I whack myself so hard my skin feels momentarily numb.

Bacon Bump passes by carrying a fiddle. He tips his hat to me with his free hand and wishes me a good evening. I didn't know that Bacon could play.

As I return my hairbrush to its place in the provision box, strapped to the wagon, I hear the sweet sawing sound of a bow across strings. Then I hear the answer of a second fiddle. The faint, thumping sound of a drum joins in.

I amble into the wagon master's campsite and watch Bacon and Agapito playing fiddles. It sounds like the instruments are locked in a spirited debate. Arikta gently pounds a round drum with his hands. As the pace quickens, the fiddle conversation becomes a furious argument that reminds me of Bobby and Wayne's fistfight in Independence. The music becomes louder and louder, and before long, a crowd forms, watching the musicians.

An Irish woman named Oona Reid steps into the wagon master's camp, turns toward the crowd, and begins to sing a song. Her brogue is so thick, I can't make out the lyrics, only just enough to understand that she is singing about a dog that bites, of all things.

The gathered crowd begins to clap along with the beat of Arikta's drum as a young woman makes her way to the front of the crowd. Berta is the oldest daughter of a German man named Wilhelm Lett. The 19-year-old girl with perfect, cornsilk blonde hair stands beside the Irish woman, and begins singing as well. Instead of facing the crowd, she faces Agapito, batting her eyelashes over her bright blue eyes. Evidently, she has decided not to pursue Schuyler Steele in the wagon next to hers.

Why should I care if the German girl moons over Agapito? I'm a happily married woman, almost old enough to be the girl's mother. I can't imagine the assistant wagon master encouraging the young girl, but if they were to fall in love with one another, it shouldn't be any concern of mine. In fact, I should be happy for my friend. But then, I think about Agapito's promise to Merced. I watch Berta and Oona's attempt to harmonize. Their heavy accents seldom seem to blend together, but Arikta, Agapito, and Bacon drown the women's voices out anyway.

When the song ends, Agapito pulls the fiddle from his chin and says to the crowd, "We thought we would practice a little bit. Do you like the music? Tomorrow evening, after supper, if the weather is good, we shall have a dance. How does that sound?"

The audience cheers, and Agapito suggests that everyone get a good night's sleep. I dawdle, lost in daydreams as everybody returns to their wagons, mesmerized by the bright night and the lingering effects of the sweet music in my ear. The full moon floods the camp with its light.

A sharp bite penetrates the thin fabric of my long-sleeved dress, and I slap my arm. Like awakening from a startling dream, I realize that I've been having unwholesome thoughts about Agapito, again. I feel my heart race as I worry that someone might read my mind, crazy as such a thought might be. Imagining his arms wrapped around me, as we stand alone together beneath the waterfall, makes the butterflies flutter in my belly.

I wonder if it is the full moon that has drawn the stinging mosquitoes out as I slap my face, again. When another insect bites below my knee, I realize that I'm alone where the crowd once stood.

With a quick blink, I notice that Boss Wheel is headed my way. I turn my head and wonder why.

He grumbles at me and says, "I must speak with you, Madame."

I should know better, but I can't help myself. "We were instructed not to speak with you, Mr. Roulette."

"Me, or my scouts, but I've noticed that you speak with them despite my request."

I nod. "I can't deny it, but they don't seem to mind."

"Why don't you mind your own business? No matter what happens, every time I turn around, there you are. Wherever there's trouble, you and your family are in the thick of it. We've got enough headaches around here. We don't need a busybody distracting us from our work."

I'm flabbergasted. "How insulting. We are kind and helpful. When something needs doing, we are there for our fellow travelers."

"And last night, that boy's paper got everybody all riled up. We don't need dissension in the ranks."

"Don't you think everybody has a right to know about the perils they might face?" I don't think I've ever stood this close to Boss Wheel before. I can't help but notice an ugly mass of damaged skin on his neck, a collection of sores that looks like a carbuncle. Hoping that a gentle tone will improve his mood, I add, "Mr. Roulette, perhaps Dr. Appleyard could take a look at your neck. Hollis or Charlotte could probably recommend a salve or something to make you feel better."

Boss Wheel's hand quickly covers his neck, ignoring my advice about his boil. He says, "I told you all to go back home, but nobody listened. And another thing, I remind you that you are a married woman. I told you the rules. My crew is not allowed to dally with the passengers. I've seen the way you look at my men."

I gasp and stomp my foot angrily. My cheeks warm, and I touch my face as if brushing an errant tendril from my cheek. "Mr. Roulette. How rude. Perhaps it is you who should mind his own business." I pivot away from him, turn slightly back toward him, and say, "Good night."

My heart pounds as I walk back to our fire. My skin burns, and I wonder if somehow the persnickety ramrod *can* read my thoughts. I toss another stick on the fire and step into the smoke that twists away from the embers, hoping to discourage the biting mosquitoes.

I grind my teeth together, thinking about Boss Wheel and his horrible accusations and insinuations. The more I think about it, the madder I get. How dare he criticize my family and me. Like everyone else, we have inalienable rights; freedom of speech and freedom of the press are two such privileges. And only God can judge our thoughts. Then, I think of gazing into Agapito's eyes, standing within his embrace during the full moon at Alcove Spring, as the sound of water splashing over the ledge completes the mood. I curse Boss Wheel under my breath.

The sun has set, and I realize that my family is tired of slapping skeeters beside the fire. It is time to prepare for bed. I take the girls with me into the woods to answer nature's call. On the way back to the wagon, we pass a wooden cross beside yet another grave. Rose turns toward the marker and says, "Goodnight, Grandmother Keyes."

I glance about and ask, "Who are you talking to, honey?"

"Don't you see the cross, Mama?"

"Oh, yes. I do." I don't know how Rose concludes that the woman or girl named Sarah is a grandmother. I understand having compassion for people we never knew, but I'm unnerved by Rose's need to speak to them as if they are friends.

Before following the girls into the wagon, I wrap my arms around my boys. I kiss Christopher on his cheek. He frowns, wipes his cheek, and disappears into the tent.

After I peck Andrew's face, he whispers, "I think something bad is going to happen, only I don't know what it is. Whenever I have a stomachache, I know that something terrible is on the way. It's not like the feeling I have when something is going to happen immediately, though." He holds his stomach as he ducks beneath the canvas. I wish I could convince him that everything will be alright.

Saturday, April 27

It feels like bug bites cover every square inch of my skin. Did I sleep at all last night? The girls are just as uncomfortable as I am. I place a hand on Dahlia Jane's warm forehead. When I check to see if Rose has a fever, she shrinks away from my touch. My wrists and ankles are red and swollen. It seems like the bug bites are layered, one upon another. On top of the sunburn, the welts itch and hurt.

Larkin grumbles and complains as he stumbles from the tent, cusses the mosquitoes, and scowls at me. When he turns away to begin his chores, I make a face back at him. It looks like the tent protected the boys from the worst of the Devil's tiny bloodsuckers. While Larkin complains about a couple of stings, I resolve to bear my misery silently.

After breakfast, we prepare to cross the Big Blue River. We are fortunate that it hasn't rained, so we don't have to wait to cross.

Stillman, and the cooper he apprenticed with back in our hometown, expertly crafted our wagon using thoroughly dried boards and tarred the seams to assure the wagon's contents remain dry during river crossings. The cooper's barrels were used to hold and transport whiskey and other liquids, so we are glad to have wagons built by such expert hands. Nevertheless, Larkin shows the boys how to elevate the wagon by placing blocks between the bed and the bolsters, so that the wagon will ride higher as we cross the river.

Before the wagons begin to traverse the Little Blue, I shuttle Jennie Banyon across on horseback, leading Blizzard through the icy river. I sputter as the bracing shock meets my skin. I trudge across the waterway on tiptoes, hoping to keep my breasts dry, yet I realize that the frigid water feels good against my swollen skin.

Once I have Jennie safely transported, I return for Esther. After retrieving Esther, I make a third trip. I've known people who fear water and drowning before, but few rival Addie's paranoia. I try to reassure her. "Jennie and Esther sit safely across the river. If the pregnant women can make it, you can too."

Addie protests as I cup my hands for her foot and heave her onto the saddle. Without my presence, Blizzard wouldn't accept another passenger. I soothe him with my voice as I lead him back into the river.

Halfway across, my feet slip on a submerged rock, and I splash into the water. I reach for my bonnet with one hand, and my other hand grabs my nose as my head goes underwater. The current pulls me downstream, and my legs tangle within my skirts until my feet find the river bottom. My hands scrape water from my eyelids, and I open my eyes just in time to see Blizzard rear, tossing my frightened friend from his back.

Addie screams before she splashes into the water. There's a commotion beneath the surface, and I shuffle along the river bottom. Her arms flail, and her legs kick indiscriminately until her head comes above water briefly. She gulps for air and takes in water, coughing as her head goes back under.

I scoop the panicked woman from the river, and her fist catches my eye. My arms tighten around her, and she screeches in fright and pain. I'm sure my grip is too tight, but I can't let go until I reach the other side.

By the time we reach the shore, Addie is crying, inconsolably. The water-logged woman is much heavier on land than in water, but she has stopped fighting. I try to assure her that she is alright as I set her back on dry land, but she throws her arms around me, clinging tightly as if her life depends on me.

"Addie, dear. I have to get my horse. You'll be fine here. Sit down beside Jennie and Esther."

I'm finally able to free myself from Addie's grip as the first wagon enters the river. Blizzard hasn't gone far, and comes to me when I whistle for him, as he has been trained to do.

I stand beside the river, dripping, shivering, and watching the wagons cross. Fortunately, the remainder of the crossing is uneventful, and our provisions are dry when Larkin and the boys reach the west bank of the Big Blue River.

As the last wagon reaches the other side, Agapito hollers, "Good work, travelers. We have a long march ahead of us today, yes? We will pass the junction of the St. Joe trail shortly before we reach Cottonwood Creek. Then we will stop for the night. Everyone is looking forward to the dance tonight, no? *Vamonos*!" Then he blasts his confounded trumpet, and the wagons begin to roll.

With no time to change into dry clothes, I climb on board and draw the bonnet closed. I manage to remove my sodden, floral dress despite the movement of the rattling wagon, and I grab for my checkered dress as the wagon hits a big rock. My body hurls forward, and my cheek hits the corner of a box. I reach a hand to my face, and it comes away bloody. I stretch for a dry washcloth, hold it to my cheek, and awkwardly climb into my clothes, one-handed. I'll have to go without my corset today, at least until it has dried sufficiently. I feel naked without it and imagine a knight without his armor as I jump from the back of the moving wagon.

I retrieve a small mirror from the provision box, and look at my wound. Despite the bloody washcloth, the injury doesn't look serious. I wonder if the long thin slice will leave a scar, but it appears superficial. Then I look at my right eye and suddenly remember when Addie's fist hit me during the river crossing. I stretch my arms and hold the mirror in my fingertips to see my whole face, all at once. I'm quite a sight to behold between my sunburn, bug bites, cracked lips, scarred cheek, and black eye. Boss Wheel need not worry. What man would be interested in a woman that looks like me? As if being one-eighth of an inch shy of six feet tall and already married with four children isn't enough to keep men from looking at me twice.

Even so, I feel much better than yesterday, when I rode all morning in the tumbling wagon. I walk a couple of miles beside the oxen before turning the whip over to Larkin and then spend the rest of the day in the saddle, chattering with Blizzard. My closest confidant is a mighty good listener, and in all seriousness, sharing troubles with a beloved animal is remarkably therapeutic.

I'm grateful for another nice campsite as we settle in at Cottonwood Creek. Hopefully, the starving insects will stay away tonight. I try to remember the last time we had fresh meat as I prepare yet another meal of cornbread, bacon, and beans. The family shovels in food without complaint. All they can talk about is the dance.

Finally, the musicians gather at The Hub. I can't help but frown at the sight of petite Berta Lett standing on a box in a fancy, pale blue dress, not a hair out of place. Oona Reid stands nearby, next to her rosy-cheeked husband, Cian, who pulls a biscuit from a shoulder bag. I don't know why Berta and Oona think we need singers at a square dance. All we need is musicians.

Evidently, dancing isn't the only thing on everyone's mind. Before the music starts, the friends we met when we signed on with Boss Wheel and

Captain Meadows argue in raised voices. The threat of outlaws attacking weighs heavy on their minds.

Bobby, the blue-shirted, dark-haired man, says, “They’re going to get you first, Wayne.”

The blond-haired man in the red shirt replies in a high pitched voice, "Is that a fact?"

"You'd better believe it."

Wayne argues, “They won’t get me.”

“You won’t see them coming.”

“Take that back.”

“No, I won’t.”

Bobby’s wife, Serena, raises her voice. “Stop it. Must you always do this? If you fight, I’m leaving.”

Serena’s brother, Wayne, dives forward, grabs Bobby’s ankles, and jerks him to the ground. The travelers gather around, cheering.

Serena shrieks, “Why do people do this? Don’t encourage them. Stop it!” In a huff, she spins around and runs toward her wagon.

I try to hold back. Maybe these young men need to work this out for themselves. After a couple of minutes of watching them roll around in the prairie dirt trying to pin each other, I’ve had enough. Shaking my head in disbelief and ignoring the voice inside my head that sounds like Boss Wheel, I step forward and lift the flailing boys to their feet. Wayne’s right fist clips my nose. I can feel blood dripping from my nostril. These boys need to be taught a lesson. I draw my fists full of shirts together, smacking Bobby and Wayne into each other, and then drop them into the dirt at my feet.

Agapito steps forward with a handkerchief and points to his nose. I thank him, wipe my nose, and pinch my nostril closed. Then I find the box that I brought, and sit down.

Boss Wheel stands at the edge of the crowd. He shakes his head judgmentally. He is too far away for me to hear his voice, but his lips move briefly, and I just know what he says, "Busybody." Fine, if that's what he wants to think. If it weren't for me, those men would still be fighting.

Drucilla pouts while her husband brushes the dust from his shirt and trousers.

Bobby sneers at Wayne and says, "If those outlaws attack the train, you'd better protect my sister."

Wayne answers, "Where's *my* sister? What if they attacked right now, huh? Don't worry about me, Bobby."

Bobby glances about, realizes that Serena is missing, and Berta says, "Your vife returnt to zee vagon."

As Bobby runs to retrieve his wife, Agapito shouts, "Let us hunt the squirrel." He's referring to the popular, Virginia Reel style dance. Couples line up in two long rows as Bacon saws his fiddle. Agapito calls commands as the columns of dancers perform the moves. When they have learned the pattern, Agapito picks up his fiddle and accompanies Bacon.

Finally, the dancers are ready for a short break. Then, pairs of couples form into squares. I watch as they spin around gracefully as Berta sings about plowing fields. For some reason, her accent doesn't seem as pronounced when she sings as when she speaks.

I'm pleased to see Rose dancing with Larkin, and they both look like they're enjoying themselves, though I haven't known either of them to be interested in dancing in the past. Andrew and Christopher dance with Berta's sisters, Katrin and Bianka, seventeen and sixteen.

The reverend's daughter, Cassie Meadows, swings back and forth between the doctor's son, Martin Appleyard, and Alvah Nye. I watch them for a few minutes. It is plain that Martin has taken to Cassie, but Cassie seems to favor Alvah, whereas Alvah doesn't seem to notice.

I check the handkerchief, relieved to see that my nose has stopped bleeding. The sun sets, crimson to the west, as the dancers twirl about, oblivious to the color in the evening sky. As the stars begin to twinkle, the moon rises full, less than half an hour after sunset.

I glance back at the twirling dancers and notice pretty young Violet Appleyard, and Addie's son, Pious Bull Jr. It's plain to see these youngsters are keen on one another. Stillman and Carter dance with Hannah and Miranda Knox, the older women from the wagon that Stillman helped repair. I wonder if Stillman and Carter would rather dance with each other than with the older women, and picture them waltzing alone on a mesa.

Exhausted, I yawn and consider returning to the wagon with Dahlia Jane. She happily dances by herself, spinning around in circles until she gets dizzy, falls, and gets up again. Instead of retiring for the evening, I stay until everyone is ready for bed. I may be tired and have a busted face, but the dance is a welcome diversion. Who knows when we'll have another night such as this? I wouldn't miss a moment of it.

Sunday, April 28

Sunday morning is cool and windy, but a day of rest is most welcome. Andrew promises that it will not rain. I still look frightful, with a scar on my cheek, a bruise on my nose, and a black eye, but Christopher tells me I look tough, like he is paying me a compliment. Larkin shakes his head and grunts, and I'm not sure *what* he's thinking.

Luella Meadows stands beside a stool at The Hub. Her fifteen-year-old son, Gideon, sits facing away from her while she cuts his hair. He talks about fishing while men gather around, waiting for their turn. I serve coffee and hand out lemon sugar cookies. Most folks want to talk about the dance and the fight last night.

Captain Meadows doesn't like it when his wife cuts hair, trims beards, and shaves men. He says, "It isn't right," but he doesn't insist that she refrain. Usually, Luella does whatever he says without question, but she says that her scissors make her happy.

I never thought about haircuts as an art form, but Luella has the same look on her face while she's snipping locks that Bacon has on his face when he paints landscapes. I love watching as she renders a scraggly-looking man handsome without much effort. When she cuts Larkin's hair, I wish that she would scrape his wiry mustache from his lip, but I know how fond of it he is. Mustaches, beards, and sideburns would be outlawed if it were up to me. I've always preferred baby-faced men to rugged-looking ones.

When I return to our wagon to launder dirty clothes, Andrew and Christopher complain that they can't find Rose. They were hoping to leave Dahlia Jane with their sister, but Rose is missing, again. I ask Larkin where Rose is, and he throws his arms up as if aggravated about being asked. "I'm sure that she'll turn up when she's done being wherever she is. That's how children are."

Ignoring Larkin, I step into the wagon master's camp and ask if they've seen Rose. Arikta tells me that he saw her about an hour ago. He points to the southwest and says she was walking along Cottonwood Creek. The serious-looking scout grows even more intense. "I can track her for you."

Recalling the proper hand signals, I put my hands flat in front of me, palms down, and move them together in a downward arc away from me. Arikta smiles and says, "You are welcome, Dorcas."

If I weren't concerned about my missing daughter, I would enjoy walking with Arikta along the creek bed. Every so often, he stops and shows me a sign that she has passed by. His trained eye doesn't miss the broken twigs and parted grasses that show where someone has been. After an hour, he points at an odd-looking structure above the creek's bank. "There," he says.

A giant, twenty-five-foot-high mound of earth stands above us. Arikta says, "My people live in these earth lodges. This one is abandoned. Do you think that Rose would go inside?"

I nod. That's exactly where I expect to find Rose. There is a short tunnel in front of the earth mound, also made of dirt. The mouth looks like a doorless entrance with long sticks propped against both sides.

We climb the creekbank, and Arikta tells me to wait. He scampers to the top of the mound. Then he flips a rigid cover from its summit and returns to my side. He looks at me and says, "Let's go in, Dorcas."

I'm amazed by what we find inside. A beam of bright light pours through the hole at the peak of the mound. Rose kneels on an animal skin in front of a circle of stones, a fire pit with no smoke or flames. She nods her head to the beat of an unheard drum. I say her name, but she doesn't seem to hear me. I've come to expect such odd behavior from her. I breathe deeply, feeling like a trespasser.

Arikta whispers as if he doesn't want to disturb Rose. "My family lived here many years ago."

I look at him, place a hand on his arm, and then look around the structure. Giant timbers form a square, like support beams, around the fire circle. Red, white, black, and yellow painted posts support a roof constructed of timbers that radiate around the structure. Behind those long poles, woven saplings hold back the dirt outside. Blankets hang around the perimeter above what looks like sleeping chambers. I think the earth lodge looks occupied rather than long abandoned.

Arikta whispers. "A lot of people lived here before the smallpox epidemic."

"I'm so sorry, Arikta. Thank goodness you survived."

"Yes. We were away, hunting buffalo when everyone here died. Very sad. We buried their bones when we returned."

Rose stands and walks around the structure. As she pauses beside each compartment, she pulls back each blanket as if listening to people behind the drapes before moving to the next. When she finishes, she returns to the center, stands in the middle of the fire circle, looks directly through the hole above, and spreads her arms wide.

Then she drops her arms, slapping her sides. She looks around, sees us, and says, "What is this place?"

Arikta answers her. "This is a Pawnee earth lodge, Rose. It was my family's home."

She says, "You have a nice family, Arikta."

Rose turns to face the exit and walks through it, returning the way she came, along Cottonwood Creek. It seems like she has forgotten that we are following her. Arikta and I look at one another, shrug, and follow Rose into camp.

When we return, Luella is still cutting hair. There seems to be no shortage of men who need a trim. Alvah sits patiently in front of Luella, and Honey sits dutifully beside him. A short distance away, Bacon Bump paints a scene of the woman cutting hair on the open prairie. I walk around and look over Bacon's shoulder. In the painting, the wagons and other travelers have disappeared, leaving only the woman, her customer, and his dog.

"What do you think, Dorcas?"

"It's wonderful, Bacon. It looks just like Luella, Alvah, and Honey. The details are just amazing. Are you finished?"

The artist stands back and looks critically upon his work before proclaiming, "Yes, I am. I may add something later, but for now, I am done." Bacon paints his signature in the corner as he asks, "Where have you been?"

I tell Bacon about the Pawnee earth lodge, and he looks at me like he's trying to imagine it, as if he is painting a picture of it in his mind. "I'd like to see it. Could you take me there, Dorcas?" He raises his eyebrow at me questioningly, and I notice that his bushy eyebrows could use a trim. "Wouldn't you like to get your hair cut first, Bacon?"

As he tries to decline, Luella insists.

With a gentle hand on Bacon's shoulder, I push him toward Luella. "While you get a trim, I'll check with Arikta and see if I can borrow a horse for you. Don't forget to ask her to trim your eyebrows for you."

I glance at Luella, who smiles and knowingly nods. The men in line grumble as she waves Bacon toward her. Alvah stands, thanks Luella, and hands her three half-dimes.

At the wagon master's camp, I'm glad to find that Boss Wheel isn't present. Agapito agrees to let Bacon borrow his golden mare, and Arikta asks whether Bacon plans to paint the earth lodge while he saddles up.

"I expect so. Is that alright?"

"Yes, I think it is good. Maybe someday, Bacon's painting will remind people what it was like to live on the prairie in the olden days. My people should never be forgotten. I will go with you."

We wait while Bacon trots to his wagon. He exchanges his completed picture for a blank canvas and a small box of supplies. I offer to carry something since Bacon will have his hands full.

As we ride off toward the abandoned lodge, I see Boss Wheel seated on his dark horse beneath a tree, frozen like a statue. I sigh. I don't expect he approves, but he doesn't move to halt us. As we pass his vantage point, I want to turn around and see if he has looked away, but I'm determined not to give him the satisfaction.

My mind wanders as we ride and I'm surprised how quickly we reach our destination. After a quick tour inside, Bacon props his canvas up against a tree trunk and begins painting.

Arikta asks, "Will this take a while?"

Bacon asks, "Could I stay for two hours?"

The scout says, "May I hunt while you paint? Do you mind if I leave you and Dorcas here?"

Bacon says he doesn't mind, but I ask if I could join the hunt. I have taken to carrying Larkin's rifle with me whenever I ride away from camp.

Arikta says there is a meadow nearby that deer frequent. After a twenty-minute ride to the west, Arikta holds up his hand, signaling a stop, and puts his fingers to his lips. I dismount, as he does, and follow him with Larkin's rifle in my right hand. We tiptoe up a short hillside and crouch when we reach the top. From a stand of small oak trees, we look down into a bright clearing, at a handful of wary mule deer.

The scout whispers, "Aim for the nearest one, the one on the left, and shoot on the count of three."

I slowly move the rifle into position, and Arikta whispers off a count. On three, we both fire. My deer collapses onto its front legs. Arikta's deer leaps forward toward us and drops to the ground after a couple of bounds.

Arikta grabs a knife from a sheath strapped to his leg and waves me forward as three lucky deer bolt safely away. He makes quick work of disemboweling the deer and drapes their bodies over the horses' backs.

When we return to the earth lodge, Bacon packs up his supplies.

Arikta asks, "Are you finished? It doesn't look done to me."

"Mostly so. What I don't have on canvas, I'll add from my memory. You can let me know if I forget anything."

When we return to camp, Agapito approaches me, and says, "I heard shots. I was just about to ride out, in case trouble had found you."

Boss Wheel follows us in. As Arikta swings the mule deer from the back of our horses and begins to skin them, Boss Wheel asks, "What's she doing here?"

Though he isn't addressing me, I answer. "Our painter wished to paint an earth lodge, so I asked if he could borrow a horse. Your crew was kind enough to lend us a horse and provide a guide. While Bacon painted, we went hunting and brought back game to share with everyone."

Boss Wheel grunts, “Mrs. Moon, in the future, leave the hunting to the men.”

“I shall not. Hunting is good practice, better than shooting at targets." I can’t be the only woman that’s ever talked back to the man, can I? I should hold my tongue, but it feels good to have the opportunity to voice a solid retort. "I should think you’d be glad to have another able shooter at hand if we are attacked.”

“It is one thing to shoot a deer and another to shoot a man. Women don’t have steady enough nerves to be of use in such situations. And another thing, I insist that your daughter remain in camp. She must not wander off by herself. I forbid it.”

I answer, “Yes, sir,” and wonder if it sounds like I am mocking him. I wish that I could prevent Rose from walking off as well. Maybe it will be easier to tell her that Boss Wheel has issued such an order.

Monday, April 29

I'm still thinking about our irritable wagon master as I prepare the family for a new week along the trail. I serve bowls of mush for breakfast, recalling how good it was to have venison on our plates last night.

When I see an opportunity to speak to Larkin within earshot of Rose but not the other children, I tell him that Boss Wheel scolded me. "He insists that Rose remain in camp and forbids the children from walking away alone. I wish we didn't have to surrender our freedom to this bossy man, but he is in a position of authority."

Rose scowls, scoffs, and turns away, mumbling. I start to follow her, and Larkin steps toward me. He says, "She heard you. Let's leave it at that."

Before I can argue with Larkin, Agapito rides toward us. He says that we will march along the Little Blue River for the rest of this week and that he will introduce us to the Platte River next week. He says that every river has its own personality, and reminds us of the differences between the Wakarusa, Kaw, Red Vermillion, Black Vermillion, Big Blue, and Little Blue Rivers.

I ask, "How many rivers lie ahead?"

Agapito thinks for a moment as if trying to count them in his head, before giving up. "Too many to count. There are many rivers, streams, and creeks but the major ones are the Platte, Sweetwater, Snake, and Columbia. Best to focus on the present, however." Then he rides down along the line.

For the first couple of hours, I trudge beside the oxen. Now that my turn is done, Larkin can decide who walks alongside the rest of the day. I plod beside the children for a while and then step back to visit with friends.

The day quickly warms to the point of being hot. I've learned my lesson, and wear my bonnet. With its drape covering my neck, I lean forward to shade my face, and begrudgingly wear gloves to protect my hands from the sun.

After stopping for dinner at mid-day, I saddle Blizzard and ride forward, a short distance ahead of the lead wagon. Beyond me, Boss Wheel sits on his horse, Clipper. I wonder how the wagon master's steed got his name.

After walking so much, it's nice to ride instead. Usually, I travel back along the chain of wagons, but today I feel contrary. I believe everyone has something about them that is good, but I don't like Boss Wheel, and I'm well aware that he doesn't like me either. Sometimes people clash when they are too similar, but that's not the situation with me and Boss Wheel. We could not be more different.

I watch the man, a couple of hundred feet ahead of me, as he pulls something from a pocket. A couple of minutes later, smoke trails over his shoulder. The man smokes most of the time, whether it's a hand-rolled cigarette, pipe, or cigar, and I wonder what makes some men do that whereas others don't.

As I plod along, I take an inventory of everything I know or have heard about this man. He's about forty-years-old, with brown eyes and black hair, just beginning to turn gray. Like his French Canadian father, he has a Brulé, Lakota wife. If Boss Wheel was born in 1810, his father must have been among the first of the trappers. His last name, Roulette, is French for Wheel, and given his occupation as a wagon master, the association with wagon wheels becomes obvious. To his face, he is called Boss Wheel, but behind his back, he's often referred to as Old Wagon Wheel.

I imagine Boss Wheel's father taking him along on trapping excursions, perhaps in the 1820s and 1830s. I've heard that in recent years, many mountain men have found guiding emigrants more lucrative than gathering and trading pelts. If he's reclusive, it must be due to his upbringing and spending so much time alone.

What are his mother's people like, and what is he like when he's among them? Given his work along the trail, I don't gather that he spends too much time with his wife.

Whenever I see Joseph Roulette, it seems that he's checking his watch, looking at a compass, gazing at a map, or looking through his spyglass. I've noticed his stiff right leg, and the abscess on his neck looks troublesome. Judging from the bags under his eyes, I guess he doesn't sleep well.

Perhaps the man's crankiness comes from caring about people. He may worry excessively about our safety but can't help that it comes across as belligerence. Or perhaps I am being charitable in my assessment.

It crosses my mind that I'd rather while away the afternoon thinking about Agapito than Boss Wheel. Then I grumble under my breath as I remember Boss Wheel's accusations about my alleged adulterous intentions.

An observant loner can be most perceptive. If there's one thing I have in common with Boss Wheel, it might be that we're both attentive to people around us. Maybe it is best that Boss Wheel sits on his horse at the edge of our settlements, and leaves Agapito to deal with the traveling village. Still, I can't help but pity the lonely man who lives beyond the fringes of humanity.

When I grow tired of observing Boss Wheel, I turn back and stop to visit with Cian and Oona, our Irish fellow travelers, from County Cork. Today, their wagon leads the train. Three teams of mules pull their wagon, rather than oxen. Though I've seen them before, I dismount Blizzard and hold a hand out to Cian, pronounced kee-an, who walks alongside carrying their infant, Aengus, pronounced ain-gus.

It's hard to understand Cian when he speaks, but I ask him questions and encourage him to speak slowly. I learn that he yearns for free land. He wants to farm, as his family did in Skibbereen, but his wife wishes to live in a quaint, safe little town.

I compliment Cian on his new haircut. After a few minutes, Cian hands me the baby and steps up onto the wagon seat. Oona passes him the reins, climbs over his body, and jumps down to walk beside me.

Their story is heartbreaking. After a couple of years of famine, beginning five years ago, death claimed every member of their families, leaving them orphaned. When distant benefactors paid for their passage, they met onboard a ship headed for America, and married before landing. Luckily, their benefactors also provided jobs when they arrived in New York. The newlyweds saved every cent they could, until they had enough money to make this overland trip.

A couple of strange things happen while I'm walking with Oona. First, I notice that she brings her hand to her forehead, like a soldier, saluting a superior officer. When I see her do it a second time, I ask, "Why do you do that?"

She explains that seeing a magpie is bad luck unless you salute it. I hadn't even noticed the presence of birds. Oona says it has become a habit, and she doesn't even realize that she does so. Then she tells me that she hopes a bird drops excrement on her from above. Such would be a harbinger of good luck, which would benefit all of us, evidently.

I've also noticed that Cian seems to be constantly eating something. While I talk with Oona, he asks her to toss him some bread. She reaches into a bag she carries at her side and throws a biscuit-sized loaf up to him.

Then, Oona asks me if I'd like to try one. I ask her about the cross-shaped marking on top, and she says the pattern releases the Devil from the bread, while it bakes. I have never thought to worry about Satan's presence in my oven. Cian nibbles at the bread, taking tiny bites, no doubt trying to preserve the loaf, and make it last. Hoping they will see it as good manners, I also take small nibbles at my bread. I compliment Oona on the tastiness of the bun.

I'm about to wish them a good day when Oona asks me if I am a witch. I'm shocked by her question. "Good Heavens! Why do you ask?"

She tells me that I'm not like other women. It's not just that I'm taller than everybody else. She also mentions the fighting boys, and my daughter, who she is sure is a witch, even if I'm not. Aengus, sleeping quietly in my arms, is proof of my otherworldly powers. Evidently, the fussy boy only sleeps when his father holds him, but the wee lad is fast asleep in my arms.

I try to laugh it off, but it is upsetting to have somebody say they think you are a sorceress. I remind myself that I don't care what people think of me. "I can assure you, my daughter is not a witch. She is just a moody child trying to adjust to changes all around her."

Despite the strange accusation, I like the Reid family, and I look forward to getting to know them better along the way. I enjoy listening to their accents and the strange way they combine words when they speak.

When the wagons circle at Rock Creek, and after everyone has had dinner, we sit by the fire and notice a new phenomenon. In the aftermath of the dance, the youngest travelers stroll the perimeter of the wagon train. It's hard to believe that anyone feels like walking when they could be resting, after marching all day. In particular, PBJ and Violet Appleyard make dozens of laps, arm in arm.

Bacon Bump has completed his earth lodge painting. I'm amazed at how lifelike the native home appears, and I can't think of any detail he missed. "What are you going to do with it, Bacon?"

Despite the fact that he has finished the painting, he still holds a brush in his hand. I suppose painters are only happy when they have the tools of their trade at hand. "I'd like to give it to Arikta. Do you think that he'd like to have it?"

I step forward and look closer at the painting. With a gasp, I look away from the portrait. "Oh, Bacon. I'm sure he would. The figure in front of the lodge, he looks just like Arikta."

The artist confirms, "That's right. He said it was his family's home, so I figured it was only right to paint him into the picture." Then Bacon tells me that he gave his haircut painting to Luella Meadows, which brought tears to her eyes. "You'd be surprised how often my paintings make people cry, but I never noticed until the last couple of years."

When Bacon asks me to accompany him to present his gift to Arikta, I nod assent. Had he not asked, I would have followed anyhow. At the scouts' camp, the artist leans his work against the master's wagon as I tell Arikta that Bacon has a gift to present him. As Bacon steps to the side, I use a hand gesture to turn Arikta toward his portrait within a landscape.

He turns, tentatively, not knowing what to expect. Then, he steps back a pace and drops to a squatting position. His hands tremble as he brings them together, steepling his fingers in front of his face. His voice chokes up as he thanks Bacon. "It is a treasure. It reminds me of so many things I thought I had forgotten." His voice trails away as he adds, "So many memories." His legs wobble as he returns to a standing position.

The humble artist simply says, "I'm glad you like it." As we leave Arikta alone with his remembrance, I wonder how he'll be able to protect the painting. What is a wilderness guide supposed to do with a fragile keepsake? Perhaps it doesn't matter if the masterpiece lasts forever. Maybe this work of art is meant to be enjoyed over a shorter period of time. Not every magnificent artifact finds its way to the hallowed walls of civilization, but I wish people in the future could look at this gem.

After the children say good night and shuffle off to bed, I tell Larkin about Bacon's painting and then I mention meeting the Reid family. When I convey Oona's accusations, Larkin smiles. “Smart girl. She confirms what I have always suspected.”

Larkin chuckles impishly and turns toward the tent without kissing me goodnight or telling me that he's joking. It shouldn't surprise me.

Tuesday, April 30

In the middle of the night, the wind begins to howl. I'm already awake when Reveille sounds. It's not raining, but dust pelts the wagon cover, and I dread today's journey. If only Rose were a witch. She could cast a spell banishing the foul zephyr from the plains.

I tie a neckerchief to my face, covering my mouth and nose, and squint as I step from the back of the wagon. I squat beside the tent and pass face coverings to Larkin and the boys. Larkin steps out, grumbles about the weather, and I follow him to retrieve the oxen.

Even without building a fire and preparing breakfast, getting ready to travel this morning is a chore. As Larkin and I lead the animals toward our wagon, I notice Andrew wrestling with the tent. The only way he can control the canvas in the wind is to roll on the ground, weighing it down as he presses it flat. Christopher struggles with Ridge, who refuses to stand still. I'm sure that dust and sand will spoil the milk, but the goat must be milked, regardless of the weather.

When we finish yoking the oxen, I retrieve Blizzard from the picket line. I make it back to our wagon with no time to spare as the trumpet signals our departure. Our wagon is third in line. As I help Rose and Dahlia Jane step down from the back of the wagon, it occurs to me that we will ride in the coveted position at the front of the train, two days from now.

The fierce, northwest wind pelts us with dust and sand. It is so windy that it is hard to walk. I worry that the powerful gusts will sweep the children away. I ask Larkin, "Please, can we let the children ride in the wagon today?"

"The oxen are overworked as it is. Now they have to pull the wagon and push against the wind. The children can walk."

"No, they can't, Larkin. Watch them. Look at how they lean into the wind, barely able to walk. You can see the misery on their faces."

"Children are stronger than you think, Dorcas."

I snatch Dahlia Jane from the ground, wrap my arms around my baby girl, and angrily walk forward, away from Larkin. Let him listen to the children complain.

Two wagons forward, I reach the Appleyard family. The more I get to know them, the better I like them. Dr. Hollis Appleyard is in his mid-forties. He talks about adventure, saving people, and searching for better cures. Charlotte is in her early forties. She's very supportive, despite being homesick, and deathly afraid of snakes. Violet walks alongside for fear of falling from the wagon. Nineteen-year-old Martin drives their mules from a bench at the front of the wagon.

Charlotte invites Dahlia Jane and me into her wagon for a visit. I turn to her husband and say, "Will it be too great of a burden on your livestock, Dr. Appleyard?"

"No, Mrs. Moon. I'm sure it will be alright, and please, call me Hollis."

He promises to reciprocate as he takes Dahlia Jane from my arms and passes her up into the wagon. Then he helps me climb aboard, though I am capable of doing so without assistance. The furious wind blows the back of my dress around, and I hope that Hollis has looked away.

I don't know how they manage to have room for two wooden chairs in the back of the wagon. Perhaps they are low on provisions. Charlotte gestures to one chair and sits in the other as Dahlia Jane climbs up onto a pile of blankets on a box.

We talk for a couple of minutes and I start to feel my anger at Larkin fading away. Charlotte speaks wistfully about the home they left behind in Richmond. Then she says, "Can you believe we've only traveled for two weeks together?" She shakes her head in disbelief. "Why, there are still almost six months yet to go."

I agree, "It hardly seems possible."

Charlotte sighs deeply and reaches for a sewing basket. "I'm making dolls for the Indians." She looks up at Dahlia Jane and asks, "Would you like a dolly too, child?"

Dahlia Jane nods wildly. Though she sits cross-legged, her body bobs up and down, overjoyed. "Can she wear a dress, just like me?"

"Yes, dear. I have three choices. They aren't exactly like your pretty pink and peach dress, but maybe you'll like one of them." Charlotte passes three, ready-made dresses up to Dahlia Jane. "Which one do you like best, sweetie?"

Dahlia Jane passes a brown dress back. "That one is ugly." A gust of wind rattles the canvas against the wagon's wooden ribs, above us, but we continue to ignore the foul weather outdoors.

Charlotte titters behind her hand as I tell Dahlia Jane that she isn't being very kind to our friend.

Charlotte looks closely at the tiny garment, and I suppose she's trying to see it through the eyes of a child. "Perhaps it is a bit drab."

Dahlia Jane apologizes, then looks back and forth, trying to decide between a bright blue dress in one hand, and a green and yellow one in her other hand. Finally, she hands them back to Charlotte. "I like this one.

The green reminds me of the prairie, and the yellow reminds me of the sunshine. Can you make her a bonnet too?"

Charlotte rifles around in her basket. "I'm way ahead of you, sweetie." She brings forth a bonnet that matches the tiny dress. "Now, I just have to finish making the doll. Which one do you think you'd like?" Charlotte passes five deflated ragdolls up to Dahlia Jane. Each has a different expression embroidered on her face.

I'm curious to see what Dahlia Jane will choose. I predict she will pick the happiest-looking doll. As suspected, she rejects the sad one and the expressionless faces. "I like this one. Her eyes look just like yours." I take note of Charlotte's vibrant, green eyes, but I'm surprised that Dahlia has chosen a doll that looks frightened. It is almost like she has seen a ghost. Dahlia Jane says, "She's beautiful, but she doesn't look like a dolly yet. She looks more like a cookie."

Charlotte laughs and reaches for a finished doll. "What do you think of her? Does she look like a little girl?"

Dahlia Jane says, "Yes, she looks like a little Indian girl."

I reach for the doll and rub the fabric of her dress between my fingers. "Why, Charlotte. It's so soft, and it looks just like deerskin."

"Yes. I'm hoping that the Indians will like them."

As we talk, Charlotte fills the canvas carcass with shredded rags and dried sage, poking and prodding the material with her fingers through a seam along the doll's spine. "How does she look now, sweetie?"

Dahlia Jane makes a face. "She's bald!"

Charlotte nods, "I know she is. We'll take care of that next. Do you think she's stuffed full enough?"

"Yes, it looks like she had a big dinner."

Charlotte asks Dahlia Jane what the doll's favorite foods are. She takes a long needle and pushes it through the coarse canvas. The wagon hits a rock and pitches us sideways. Charlotte pokes her fingertip with the needle. "You would think I could learn to use a thimble when I sew in the moving wagon. What does it say about me that I make the same mistake, over and over again?" Then she finishes stitching up the seam. Charlotte interrupts Dahlia Jane's long list of the doll's favorite foods and asks, "What color hair would you like?" Dahlia Jane picks a blondish brown color, similar to her own.

I'm amazed at how quickly the ghostlike canvas has transformed into a lifelike, little girl. As Charlotte finishes sewing the yarn hair onto the apparition, she says, "Would you like to dress her?"

Dahlia Jane nods enthusiastically. "Would I ever?!"

Charlotte passes the finished doll over her shoulder. "Let me know if you need any help, dear."

"Yes, ma'am."

While Dahlia Jane works on dressing the ragdoll in her green and yellow dress, Charlotte picks up a stoic-looking doll shell. When she finishes stuffing it, she sews long, straight hair onto it and adds a beaded headband. Dahlia exclaims, "She looks just like an Indian princess."

"Really, sweetie? Have you ever seen an Indian princess?" Dalia Jane shakes her head, and Charlotte says. "Me neither. I hope we got it right."

Dahlia Jane asks, "Can I have her too?"

"No darling, this doll is for a little Indian girl. I'm sorry, dear."

"I understand."

Charlotte cups Dahlia Jane's tiny cheek in her palm. "You're such a good girl." Then she looks back at me, sighs mournfully, and says, "I miss having little ones around. Teenagers aren't like the little darlings." Charlotte looks back at Dahlia Jane, and asks, "Are you going to name her?" Dahlia Jane assures the woman that she will once she thinks up a perfect name.

I prod, "What do you say to Mrs. Appleyard, Dahlia Jane."

"Thank you, ma'am. Thank you so much. She's beautiful, and I love her. All she needs now is a home, just like me. Someday, she'd like to live in a house."

Charlotte reaches a hand back and taps Dahlia Jane's knee. "I know just how she feels, sweetie. Someday, she will. You tell her to be patient, and her dreams will come true."

"Yes, ma'am."

Charlotte twists her body so she can look into Dahlia Jane's eyes as she asks, "Other than having a house, what else does she dream of?"

Dahlia Jane answers as if she were speaking to another little girl, rather than a grown woman. "I don't know, ma'am. We just met, and she hasn't told me yet."

Charlotte pats the top of Dahlia Jane's head. "Oh, I see. Well, please let me know when you find out."

I'm amazed at how quickly the morning has passed. Despite the rocking wagon, I've almost forgotten where we are as the wheels slow to a stop. I don't enjoy sewing, but it has been wonderful to sit and talk with Charlotte, and it warms my heart to see Dahlia Jane squeeze her new ragdoll, lovingly to her chest.

Hollis meets us as I prepare to step down, offering his hand in assistance. Before returning to my own wagon, I turn to Charlotte. "You're very kind, and we've had a wonderful morning."

Our midday stop is abbreviated, which is too bad because Fremont Springs looks most inviting. The swirling winds dictate another meal of biscuits and water. Despite the wind, I dump our barrel and fill it with fresh water from the spring. The children each take a couple sips of sandy goat's milk before the wagons roll again, without complaint, but Larkin grumbles about the grit and frowns at the biscuits. The upside of a short midday stop is the potential to reach the end of the day sooner.

After an afternoon of being pelted by the relentless winds, I'm glad when Agapito rides by on his way toward the Appleyard's wagon, shouting, "Prepare to circle up." The wagon master's wagon stops first, points its tongue outward, and we pull up into position behind it. Agapito leads the Appleyard's wagon around until it is at the end of the procession. Tomorrow, they'll ride at the back, rather than the front.

After a day of windblown sand, it seems fitting that we would find ourselves camped near a tributary called Big Sandy Creek. As I lead the children toward it to gather wood, I stop and watch as Rose wanders off a short distance. She walks up to a row of graves, squats in front of the first one, and pats the ground like she's comforting an ailing person.

I send Andrew and Christopher forth to gather wood and remain nearby, watching as Rose visits each grave. It is as if she feels the loss of people she never met. The presence of their graves is a grim reminder of the many perils we must face. I look back at the twin ruts along the trail. When we set out from Independence, I thought of the journey as exciting and full of adventure, but now I wonder whether the sinister trail leads only to misery and misfortune.

When Rose finishes at the last of the six graves, she wanders toward the nearest tree, and gathers fallen branches. I wonder whether she says prayers at each grave, which I can't help but admire, even as I hope that her preoccupation with death will soon pass. Larkin insists it will.

Wednesday, May 1

THE NEW DAY BEGINS cold, and the wind chills my bones like the last day of February rather than the beginning of May. How long can the howling continue? After yesterday, I would expect today to be calmer, but if anything, the wind blows even more furiously.

Larkin is already up and about as I climb from the back of the wagon. Despite the clamor of tools banging against the wagon's side and the howling wind, my husband's growls catch my ear and set me on edge. I hand him a couple of biscuits for his breakfast, and he swears at me. I say, "I know, Larkin. I don't like it any more than you do. I'll help you yoke the oxen after I tempt a snake. Where's Rose?"

He looks exasperated, throws his hands in the air, and says, "How should I know?"

I pluck Dahlia Jane from the back of the wagon and glance about for a place that might offer us some privacy. Something catches my eye, and I walk toward Big Sandy Creek.

There's Rose, stretched out on the ground, stiff as a board with her arms crossed over her chest, surrounded by the graves she visited yesterday. She's on her back, just as if she were stretched out in a coffin. My heart leaps in fear. It's not the first time I've worried that Rose is going mad, and I don't know what to do. Larkin keeps telling me to let Rose work out whatever she's going through, but I can't help thinking that she needs to talk to somebody. But who?

I glance around, and we are not alone. A couple of our hunters stand nearby. Galusha Gains and Samuel Grosvenor are both from Portage, Pennsylvania. A prominent sneer curls Galusha's lip, and Samuel rubs his chin as they watch Rose. In the past, I have heard Galusha talk about wanting to shoot Indians, and buffalo—as many of each as possible, and Samuel always seems to be nearby, a most disagreeable sidekick. I wish they were somewhere else this morning.

As I get closer, I realize that Rose's eyes are closed. If I didn't know better, I would think she were dead herself. She barely seems to breathe. Her stringy hair blows around her face, and the hem of her burgundy dress rustles at her ankles. Otherwise, she is motionless. I whisper, "Rose, honey." I glance toward Galusha and Samuel. They have stepped a bit closer. A little louder, I repeat, "Rose, honey."

She rises slowly, "Yes, Mama?" She's calm, almost serene, which is unusual for Rose, whose morning demeanor is regularly unpleasant. I tell her we'll be leaving soon, and she says, "Thanks, Mama. I'll be along in a minute."

I say, "Alright, Rose," and continue onward. When we reach the shelter of a large tree and a medium shrub, I turn and see Rose walking back toward the wagon. Then, I watch as Galusha and Samuel step forward and inspect the graves. As they face each other, I can see Galusha speaking to Samuel, even from a distance.

Dahlia Jane tugs at my dress. I hold up a finger and shush her. "Just a minute, dear."

Galusha's body rocks from side to side as he rants, and Samuel nods, evidently agreeing with everything his friend says. I can only imagine what they're saying. Finally, the nosy men move toward their wagons, seven and eight positions behind ours. I think of Boss Wheel and remember him calling *me* a busybody. Perhaps the ramrod should speak to Galusha and Samuel.

My mind is on the day ahead, on the way back to camp. It's hard to fathom that it can be so cold or the wind can blow so hard on such a bright, sunny day.

After walking with the oxen for a couple of hours, I hand Larkin the whip and say, "I'll be back later."

He scowls at me and says, "Where are you going now? Why don't you stay put for a change?"

I mash my teeth. I do more than my share of tending the oxen, in addition to keeping everybody fed and clothed. I glower at him and say, "Alright, Larkin." After a silent half an hour walking beside him, waiting for him to say something, I repeat, "I'll be back later."

He throws his hands up in the air and looks toward the heavens. I scoop Dahlia Jane into my arms and walk away from Larkin without looking back.

At the next wagon, Dahlia Jane shows Stillman and Carter her new doll, who remains unnamed. Carter kneels beside my girl, looks closely at her toy, and tells Dahlia Jane that her doll reminds him of his mother. I rustle the man's hair like he's ten instead of twenty, as he tells Dahlia Jane that his mother was named Dolly.

Next, we make our way to the Banyon wagon. Bess admires Dahlia Jane's doll and says she wishes she had one just like it. Dahlia Jane tells Bess that she will ask Mrs. Appleyard to make her one.

Jennie looks like a stick figure attached to a pumpkin. She never complains, but I can read the effects of a difficult pregnancy on her face. I ask, "Is there anything I can do for you?"

She glances at me briefly, then looks to her side. She says, "Cobb takes good care of us. Thank you just the same." Her adoring expression fades as she looks back at me. She raises an eyebrow and says, "I just have to keep going, Dorcas."

Addie and Esther step forward from a nearby wagon. I always avoid asking Esther how she feels since she tends to fuss. Instead, I say, "How much longer until the baby is due, Esther?"

Esther frowns. "I guess it could be any time now. The baby can't come soon enough if you ask me." She complains about being uncomfortable, but the sturdy woman makes poor Jennie look all the more frail in comparison.

When Esther pauses, I address Jennie, "How about you? Do you have much longer to wait?"

She raises an eyebrow and forces a smile. "I've got another month to go, maybe longer. I figure the baby will come in the middle of June."

I say, "I wonder where we'll be by then."

Jennie says, "Me too," but it's not like either of us knows much about what's ahead of us.

Esther changes the subject. "I hear that Galusha Gains has been complaining about Rose."

I'm taken aback. "What do you mean? Who did he complain to, and what did he complain about?"

Esther says, "I was visiting with the hot-headed kids and their wives. Their wagons are right behind Addie's wagon, you know. Serena Bond says that Galusha Gains, whose wagon is next after theirs, has been running his mouth. He has complained to Boss Wheel, and anybody that will listen, saying that the Devil has claimed your daughter. He says that Rose walks around in a trance and doesn't hear anybody when they speak to her."

Esther places a hand on her hip, turns to me, and says, "What kind of man talks about a young girl that way?"

When I proceed to respond, I realize that my mouth has been hanging open. "How cruel. What business is it of his? Rose is just a moody kid with some kind of worry about death. Larkin says to leave her alone, and that she'll outgrow it."

Esther turns to Addie. "Evidently, Galusha has also complained about your son. The way that boy and the doctor's daughter carry on." As if for dramatic effect, Esther nods and pauses." Serena and Drucilla said that Galusha followed PBJ and Violet to the river, Monday night, and saw them kissing. When he reported it to Captain Meadows, Galusha claimed that their hands were all over each other, that the young man groped the poor girl, and if he hadn't interrupted them, there's no telling what might have happened." I can feel my eyes rolling angrily in my head. Then I think of Stillman and Carter. Thank goodness Galusha Gains hasn't stumbled upon them.

Addie angrily huffs and says, "One night, I saw Galusha smack his wife, Pamela. He whacked her with the back of his hand, and she fell to the ground. I was carrying a pail of water, and the sight stopped me in my tracks. Then he kicked her bottom. The poor woman sobbed, and I dropped my bucket. Galusha looked up, saw me standing there, and scowled at me. He asked me what I was looking at. I grabbed my pail, and ran back to our wagon. And that's not all. Their neighbor, Samuel, is a drunk. I don't know how many times I've seen him pulling on a jug. I'm not one to spy on people, but I couldn't help but notice his wife taking nips as well."

I glance at Jennie and decide she is too tired to go on. I've heard enough gossip for one day. I hope Jennie won't be angry, but I approach Cobb anyhow. He greets me with a bright, toothy smile. When I tell him that

Jennie has grown peaked, he thanks me. I take the whip from his hand and suggest he help her into the back of the wagon. Then, when Cobb reappears, I return to my family.

When the day ends, and the wagons circle, Agapito points north. Larkin nods and leads the oxen in the direction that Agapito signals. Andrew and Christopher jump up and down, slapping their hands together in the air. They are looking forward to leading the wagon train tomorrow.

Covertly, I follow Rose, picking up sticks for the fire as I go. She floats like a cloud from grave to grave. The first several are obvious, with earth mounds and crosses. Others barely look like graves anymore, and I would overlook them if it weren't for Rose pausing as she passes by. Why does it seem that there are graves everywhere we camp? How many people have perished on the way to Oregon? It's frightening to contemplate. I've gathered more sticks than I can comfortably carry and have counted ten graves by the time Rose completes her tour.

The sun sets quickly and the wind still whips. As I climb into the wagon, Agapito rides into camp. He tells Larkin, "Get to sleep early. You stand watch at midnight, and tomorrow will be a long day."

I fight to fall asleep but can't stop thinking about Galusha. If anybody should mind their own business, it is him. I shudder to think what will happen if I catch him beating his wife. I can't be trusted to mind my own business.

Thursday, May 2

When the blasted horn honks, I realize that I must have fallen asleep. The cold north wind blasts sand into the wagon, and I rub my eyes, wondering how many days in a row the evil, howling wind can blow.

Our wagon leads the train today, which means we must be ready to roll on nine blasts of the trumpet. As I climb to the ground, Arikta runs by. "No fires today."

I sigh, feeling tired before the day even begins. Larkin must be even more exhausted, and I hope he managed to get a few hours of sleep before midnight.

Late in the afternoon, we approach The Narrows of the Little Blue River. On one side, the trail skims the river's edge. On the other side, high bluffs funnel the procession into single file, forcing pedestrians behind their wagons rather than alongside. Dahlia Jane rides in the wagon while Rose leads Ridge, ahead of the oxen. In anticipation of an afternoon ride, once we reach the other side of the passage, I lead Blizzard with his reins in my hand. Andrew and Christopher walk just ahead of me, also behind our wagon. They're still thrilled about being at the front of the string of wagons.

As we approach the gap between the river and the bluffs, we're surprised by a sudden boom, immediately followed by a rumbling sound. A sharp jolt jabs the ground. The quake causes the oxen to bellow, and they begin to run, even as the earth shakes beneath them.

There's a crashing sound above us. As I turn to look upward, I see a boulder bounding down the bluff. Everything seems to be happening so fast that it doesn't seem real, yet even in fractions of seconds, thoughts come fast.

I scream at the boys, "Run."

They race around the wagon and escape through The Narrows, just ahead of the oxen as Larkin cracks the whip. I cringe, hearing the sound the whip makes when it strikes the oxen rather than the air above them. Larkin screams at the beasts, and I stop in my tracks.

Blizzard rears, pulling the reins from my hands. He bucks, and then runs wild.

I shuffle my feet and back into Stillman and Carter's oxen as the rock bounds toward our wagon.

Distraction causes me to stumble. Our neighbors' ox steps on my dress with his front hoof. Then he tramples my foot with his back hoof, and I roll off to the right.

I sit up fast, and even from the ground, I can see the boulder's trajectory. It's almost upon us now. It pitches from side to side, unpredictably. It could hit me, but it's too late to try to outrun it now. I scream as it takes a final bounce into the back right wheel of our wagon, mere yards ahead.

Dahlia Jane howls as the rolling stone comes to a stop with a cracking crunch, sending spokes and splinters into the air, as our oxen drag the wagon a few more feet. Our prairie schooner comes to a skidding halt, blocking the narrowest spot on the trail. Destructive as the boulder is, I'm glad it's not bigger than a water barrel. It's certainly big enough to wreck our wheel.

Stillman rushes to my side and helps me to my feet. I almost fall to the dirt when I put my left foot on the ground. Stillman's face twists as if he knows how my foot feels. Perhaps he's mirroring the look on my face.

I limp forward and Stillman follows. My screeching child calls to me from the wagon. I limp forward, fast as I can, and try to ignore the fiery pain in my left foot.

"I can't find Dolly, Mama. I think she might be hurt." Dahlia Jane pounds my chest with her tiny fists as I pull her from the back of the wagon.

Stillman jumps into the wagon as Carter arrives with the wagon jack.

Galusha arrives at the scene just ahead of his pal, Samuel. It occurs to me that his stomping feet could cause another boulder to roll down upon us as he unleashes a tirade of complaints. "What the blazes is going on now?"

Samuel titters at his side, encouraging him to go on.

"I should have known that this would happen with *you* leading the train." As Carter cranks the wagon up a couple of notches along the jack, Galusha kicks dirt with his boot and says, "Now look what you've gone and done. It figures you'd block the trail and ain't nobody gonna be able to get by you. It's gonna be dark before we circle up tonight."

Behind them, Horace Blocker, our expedition's foremost naysayer, cracks his knuckles and gripes, "I'll be shocked if any of us survive this accursed expedition. What's the point of going on?"

Stillman dives from the wagon with the doll in hand. Its right arm is torn and almost severed, making Dahlia Jane scream again. He kneels before her, "Don't worry, she can be sewn up, good as new."

Galusha pipes up. "Don't we have more important things to worry about than a child's plaything? Get a move on."

Agapito trots up beside Galusha on his golden mare. He glances about quickly, assessing the situation, and begins shouting. "Carter, run back to my wagon. You'll find a spare wheel in the back. Roll it here." The wagon master's rig is last in line today.

Carter blasts off at a run. Agapito turns slightly and shouts, "Stillman, get Schuyler Steele. Galusha, remove the wheel from the wagon."

Galusha makes a face at Agapito. "That ain't my wagon. Let someone else do it." He points at Larkin by thrusting his face forward, not even bothering to lift a finger to point.

Larkin steps toward the wagon, removes the nut at the hub, and shakes the wheel from the wagon. Agapito inspects the corner of the wagon bed, and the remains of the wheel. "That is a well-built wagon. As for the wheel, maybe we can salvage the iron, but the wood is finished, no?"

The ground rumbles again, mildly in comparison, and the gathering crowd looks up at the bluff as dirt and small stones skittle down the hillside.

Horace grumbles. "If the trail don't get us now, it'll get us later. If we somehow manage to survive the trail, those outlaws will finish us for sure." With a sigh deep enough to cause another earthquake, Horace turns around and heads back to his wagon.

Galusha says, "I dunno about all that, but I say we don't let *them* lead the train again."

Agapito says, "It is not their fault. There is no curse. It is just bad luck that we happened to be here at this moment. We will have a new wheel on that wagon, and be on our way in no time, yes? Return to your wagons and take a short break." Then he smiles as if the thought of tooting his horn delights him and says, "Listen for the signal. We will roll soon."

Galusha and Samuel turn back toward their wagons. Agapito speaks to those who remain. "I have never felt an earthquake before. Has anybody else?" He glances about, sees everyone shaking their heads, and says, "What a story you will have to tell, yes?" Then he suggests that Larkin grease the axle while we wait.

Carter arrives with the spare wheel just as Larkin finishes with the grease. Agapito lifts the replacement into place, and Carter tightens the nut. Agapito rubs his hands together, indicating that he's pleased with how quickly we finished the job.

Agapito takes a couple short steps, drops to a squatting position in front of the boulder. He clenches his jaw, places his hands on the stone, and pushes it forward. Sweat beads on his forehead, and he groans as he rolls the rock away from the trail. With a deep breath as he stands, Agapito brushes his palms together again and steps toward Rio to retrieve his bugle.

Larkin cracks the whip, and our wagon begins to roll. I think of Rose and the goat, Andrew, and Christopher, on the other side of the Narrows, and then I remember my horse. I start to panic, bring my fingers to my lips and send a shrill whistle into the air. I'm relieved to hear a breathy nicker nearby. When Dembi Koofai rides his Appaloosa forward, leading Blizzard, I make the hand sign that conveys my thanks. Stillman helps Dahlia Jane back into the wagon. I wince as I place my injured left foot in the stirrup, grimace, and throw my right foot over the Andalusian's rump.

I revel in the glory of proving the naysayers wrong when the wagons circle near the river about a mile and a half away from the bottleneck at The Narrows.

My good mood is short-lived. After dinner, Captain Meadows, Wade Crouse, and Travis Latham drop by for an unexpected visit. Are they passing along the train visiting with everyone, or is it only our camp that interests them today?

Larkin stands, shakes their hands, and the men exchange pleasantries. Remembering when Travis Latham complained about his tooth the last time the Committee came calling, I ask the man, "How's your toothache, Mr. Latham? Better, I hope."

He nods. "Yes, ma'am. Thank you."

Captain Meadows curtly says, "I'll get right to the point. We've had some complaints. I'd like to speak with your daughter."

Larkin says, "What for? What complaints?"

Captain Meadows tilts his head forward, and his eyebrows tighten. "Strange behavior, for one thing." He turns away from Larkin, and addresses me. "Bring the girl to me, Mrs. Moon."

I feel my hands ball up into fists. I'd love to deck the preacher. I can vividly imagine knocking the man to the ground.

Larkin turns Captain Meadows away from me with his hand on the man's shoulder. "Our children are none of your concern, Captain. I'm going to have to ask you to leave."

Rose steps forward as if summoned. "It's okay, Mama. Did you want to see me, Captain Meadows?"

I look at Larkin. The murderous intent in his eyes reflects my anger at the unwelcome intervention. I'm proud of Larkin for challenging Captain Meadows, and then I look back at Rose, who doesn't seem to wither from the man's scrutiny either.

Captain Meadows clears his throat. "Yes, young lady. I've had several complaints about you."

"My name is Rose."

"Rose, then." He clears his throat again and continues. "Why do you insist on walking off by yourself? It isn't right or proper for a girl your age to be alone in the wilderness."

"I know. I get to daydreaming, and I can't help myself. I'll try to be more careful."

I'm proud of Rose and surprised at how well she handles Captain Meadows' inquiry. The moody girl doesn't roll her eyes or protest his questions like she does when I speak to her. Fortunately, Rose seems remarkably lucid.

"Ahem. Yes, Rose. We've also had complaints about your strange behavior."

"What do you mean, Reverend Meadows?"

"Well, take this morning, for instance. You were seen on the ground beside strangers' graves, and people say that you are always talking to yourself."

"I like to pray for them. Is it wrong to pray for the dead, Reverend?"

"Of course not," he answers sharply. "But what about you being on the ground?"

"Isn't it proper to kneel when you pray?"

"Kneeling is one thing. Stretching out on the ground like a corpse is another matter."

"I thought it would make their souls more comfortable if I lay like they do."

Reverend Meadows grumbles. "I should think that kneeling would be sufficient, young lady. I've also been told that you walk about like you are in a trance."

"I guess I can be absent-minded sometimes, sir. I'll try to be more careful."

"Well, yes. See that you do."

"Is there anything else, Reverend Meadows?"

"No. No, that's about it, I suppose. Just stay with the train, you hear?"

"Yes, sir." Rose glances at me and smiles slightly. I admire how she got the better of Captain Meadows, but I'm unsure what she's saying to me with her expression.

Without looking at his fellow Committeemen, Captain Meadows says, "Come along, men." Before leaving, he glances at Rose with a look that warns that he will be watching.

Friday, May 3

My legs drop from the wagon into a dark foggy morning. When my left foot hits the ground, pain cripples my ankle and I remember Stillman and Carter's trampling ox. My leg gives way beneath me, and my body crashes to the ground.

With a strong push, I climb to my legs and limp into the dark woods along the creek to search for kindling. A stick cracks in the woods, and my arm hairs bristle. I turn and see a gray figure approaching through the mist, and quake in fear. Blood floods my veins like the rivers when it rains. Then I hear Rose's voice. "Good morning, Mama." As she passes by, I watch her disappear behind me as she makes her way back to camp.

When I return to our wagon, the boys stretch and yawn. Larkin grumbles. "We'll be riding drag and eating everybody's dust today. Better get the neckerchiefs out."

Christopher says, "I wish we could ride in front every day. I don't care about the dirt. I just like being first."

Andrew replies. "Well, we have to take turns. It is only fair. Today, it is Stillman and Carter's turn to lead the train."

Christopher says, "It's just disappointing, slowly working your way to the front, and then you only get to stay there for one day."

Larkin complains. "I don't know about the rest of you, but I could use a day off. It feels like we've been walking forever, like a herd of buffalo, always on the move. We're men, not beasts, after all."

I'm grateful when the trumpet signals our departure. I've heard enough moaning and complaining. As I limp along beside the oxen, it strikes me that if anybody has a reason to complain, it's me. Yet, despite a sunburn, black eye, and gimpy foot, I'm still reveling in a journey that reminds me of Odysseus's epic voyage.

The fog burns away quickly, leaving a cloudless sky. The air is eerily still. After so much wind, tranquility would seem a welcome blessing, but as the temperature climbs toward eighty degrees, it is hard to believe that it is still early May. We are limited to extremes on the prairie. We must endure gale-force winds, or no wind at all. I feel as if doing so without complaint builds character.

After driving the oxen most of the morning, I saddle up after our midday break. Knowing that Boss Wheel stands beyond the lead wagon, I guide Blizzard in the opposite direction, beyond the last wagon, and turn slightly toward the north. Despite the chance of burning my skin again, I remove my bonnet and stuff it into the hole behind the saddle horn. I shake my noddle, and free my frizzy hair.

Blizzard tosses his head. Instead of tightening my hold, I loosen the reins and squeeze my legs together. On my signal, Blizzard takes off at a gallop, enjoying the freedom that open spaces provide. Who cares what Boss Wheel or The Committee thinks? I need to escape the confines of their authority as much as the Andalusian does.

After ten minutes, I slow to a trot. In the distance, I see a mounted figure. When you're far from the protection of the wagon train, strangers mean trouble, especially in unsettled territory. I'm sure that the rider sees me since he's headed directly toward me at a leisurely trot. I convince myself that a foe would charge at a gallop. Then I see Honey, the black Labrador retriever bounding along beside Alvah. I try to recall the name of the horse he's mounted on. I rarely forget the names of animals, or people. It comes to me. Monsoon!

I'm relieved to see the young man. When he reaches me, I ask, "How did you get away from your wagon this afternoon?"

Alvah laughs and says, "I know a young fella by the name of Christopher. He's a hardworking boy, and my stock seems to like him. A half-dime buys me an hour away. Unfortunately, the plains are quiet today. I haven't found any game."

"That's too bad. It's always nice to have meat. I like biscuits, but sometimes it's good to have something else." Alvah says he's headed back, and I ask him if he minds having company.

Alvah shares hunting stories as we trot slowly back toward the west. As he speaks, I'm aware of darkening skies. Black clouds overtake the gray ones and appear to boil in the atmosphere. The wind picks up speed and seems to change direction by the second until it blows from every direction, simultaneously.

Alvah points toward the river and gallops away. The wind howls in my ear. I press my heel into Blizzard's side, and he tears off after Alvah.

Near the river's edge, I pull the reins, and Blizzard skids to a stop near Alvah. I follow the man's lead, quickly strip my gear from the horse's back, remove his bridle, and slap his rump. I mutter a quick prayer under my breath for the animal's safety. How far off is the wagon train? I thought we made it most of the way back.

Alvah smacks my shoulder to get my attention. "Find a tree. Wrap your arms around it and hold on like your life depends on it. It just might."

Blizzard whinnies loudly, rears up, paws the air, and gallops away. Alvah's horse follows, evidently trusting Blizzard's instincts.

The fickle storm changes its personality constantly. Banks of clouds at various elevations roll across each other. The sun appears to peek through from beyond the horrific chaos from time to time. Shape-shifting clouds tumble haphazardly across the sky. The fierce wind pelts my face, but holding on to my tree is not a challenge, at least not yet. I wonder whether I should close my eyes to keep them clear of dust and dirt. Ultimately, I can't help but watch the storm through slit eyes, worrying about the wagons and my children.

The clouds begin to twirl, rotating in a circular movement. Instead of remaining in the sky, part of the clouds drop from the heavens and touch the earth. It looks like a giant rope or a thick snake, bending and twisting from top to bottom. It dances on the plain, constantly changing its movement. At the same time, the vortex is stationary, as if it can't decide which direction to travel.

Time is hard to judge in moments like this. It could be minutes, or it could be hours. As we watch, the spinning monster gathers strength. It was frightening enough when it first formed, but its menacing presence is overwhelming now. It is dark, ugly, and looks to be a mile wide. I pray it will stay where it is or move away from us.

Lightning cracks illuminate the twister at its fringes. Beyond the angry column, its outer orbit sucks dirt and debris from the ground. It is often challenging to find enough branches when looking for fodder for our fire, but the tornado seems to have no problem gathering fuel to add to its oppressive mass.

If it moves this way, we're goners. How could we grip a tree strongly enough to prevent getting pulled into the angry beast?

Then, another swirling cone appears in the sky, a couple of miles away, to the right of first. The new one moves more dramatically, as if impatient to be going somewhere. And then, a third tornado appears on the opposite side of the gargantuan cyclone.

I'm increasingly aware of the sound of the storms. At first, it sounds like a deep rumble. I imagine a herd of stampeding buffalo, and the sound they might make. It grows louder, and the sound reverberates within my core. Above the din, there is an angry roar. I have never heard a mountain lion, but the rumbling sound makes me think of a giant, otherworldly cat.

I can easily imagine that this scary situation can get a whole lot worse, yet I'm surprised when it starts to rain. The rain lasts but seconds before changing to tiny pellets of ice. They don't just fall from the sky, but seem driven like bullets from a rifle.

Suddenly the tiny ice pellets become large——hail! The slight sting of ice pellets now feels like a constant barrage, making me wish I could cover my head while holding onto the tree. It feels like I'm in a fistfight against an unseen gang of hundreds.

Then, as quickly as it began, the hail subsides. I feel relief in the aftermath, but then realize that the roar is even louder than it had been. The family of tornadoes remains, and the patriarch has grown even larger. Could it be two miles wide? I can't believe they're stuck in the same place. How long can the sky roil with such intensity?

What next? As that thought crosses my mind, the devastating answer immediately follows. Stationary no longer, the three funnels begin to move. And they're headed in our direction.

I no longer care to watch. I slam my eyes shut, pray for Blizzard, and clutch the tree with all my might.

Fury descends. I visualize being ripped from my anchor, flying through the air, and tumbling randomly. Then, I imagine the storm flinging me to the ground, shattering every bone on impact.

The debris from the storm batters my back. I'm glad, at least, that the tree protects my stomach.

This can't be the two-mile-wide tornado ripping through us. How could we survive that? Maybe it's one of the smaller members of the family, or perhaps we are between the storms. I don't intend to open my eyes until the wind stops blowing, if it ever does.

When it finally subsides, I open my eyes, release my hold on the tree, and stumble to my feet. As the twisters skitter off to the east, Rose walks from the direction of the departing storm. Her hair whips and spins about her head. I run toward her and throw my arms around her, gripping her tightly, like the cottonwood tree I clung to a short while earlier.

"Rose, honey." I stutter incredulously, "How did you survive the storm? You must be frightened. Are you alright?"

She pulls away from my embrace and looks into my face like she doesn't recognize me. The skin beneath her right eye twitches. I've never noticed this facial tic before. Rose takes a few steps backward, stretches her arms out, and spins like she is pretending to be a tornado, herself. Then she takes a few dizzy steps toward me and falls to the ground, laughing like a girl Dahlia Jane's age. She says, "That was a mean storm."

Alvah steps toward Rose, reaches his hand toward her, and pulls her to her feet. "You could say that again. We'd better get back." He looks around, no doubt searching for our horses. Then he shouts, "Honey. Where are you, girl? Come, Honey!" He places his hands beside his cheeks and repeats his call.

I put my fingers to my lips and whistle loudly. A distant neigh answers, and I hear hoofbeats on the prairie as Blizzard gallops toward us, Monsoon running alongside.

A nearby whimper catches my ear, and I point at a pair of rocks. Alvah's hunting partner is holed up in a small space between the boulders. In a soothing voice, Alvah reassures her, "It's okay, Honey. You can come out now."

The Labrador retriever tentatively crawls from its temporary den, and then quickly runs to her master's side. After a brief rendezvous, Alvah helps Rose climb onto Blizzard's back, behind me. The whole way home, I think about how Rose walked undaunted through a storm that blew so hard that Alvah and I had to lock our arms around trees. Finally, I convince myself that she must have come upon it as it was losing strength, and changing course, and we only noticed her approach at the last moment as she turned direction and appeared to be walking directly from the heart of the storm.

When we return to camp, Larkin shouts at me. He's so mad, his body shakes. With his fists in the air, he says, "Where were you? We could have been killed. What if those tornadoes hit the wagons? I felt so hopeless, not knowing where you were. It was all I could do to keep everything from blowing away. Don't you know enough not to ride out into a storm?"

"Larkin, there wasn't a storm when I rode out."

"When you rode out? What about Rose? Didn't you ride out together?"

I decide it is better not to answer. "Could you help Rose down?" When Rose is safely on the ground, I sweep my right foot over Blizzard's rump and slide off. I can understand why Larkin is angry, but I'm not in the mood to bicker or fight. It's better not to think about him at times like this. He'll simmer down and forget it before long, he always does.

Though it's only early afternoon, Arikta rides by with a quick word to inform us that we'll be stopping early today. Larkin is still angry and doesn't speak to me all afternoon. I dedicate the rest of the day to laundry and baking, hobbling around. Then I set out to check on our neighbors.

Evidently, the storm didn't threaten the wagons. Alvah and I were much closer to the tornado's path. I try to imagine what would have happened if the two-mile-wide twister had crashed into the wagon train, and cringe at the thought of the devastation. Perhaps everyone would have been killed.

At the Banyon's camp, with her husband's arm protectively draped over Jennie's shoulder, she says, "I wasn't worried. Cobb would have protected us."

I find the Bull family praying, conveying their thanks for having survived. With my arrival, they stand, and Addie excitedly tells me about the tornadoes, as if she were the only one that saw them, and it happened long ago.

Esther Bump remains highly agitated, muttering and waddling about doing chores in an unorganized fashion. Beyond their campfire, Bacon works at an easel, and I wonder what he is painting. Robbie and Ellen play quietly beneath the wagon. I ask Esther if I can help her with anything, but I can't comprehend her response. Instead, I walk over to visit with Bacon.

I'm astonished by the image he has captured. Three funnels twist like angry ghosts from the prairie, the wide one in the middle has a human face, and a small girl in a burgundy-colored dress stands in front of the tornadoes, her arms raised above her head. I look more closely at the screaming face in the swirling gray storm. I can't help but gasp in recognition. He looks like a man from our hometown who died last year under questionable circumstances. I look at Bacon with a question on my mind, but I decide not to ask it. Why is Armand Bartholomieux's face painted onto the ferocious cyclone?

Bacon asks, "What do you think?"

I shake my head. "It's most disturbing, Bacon."

He shrugs as Esther approaches. I can't help thinking that her baby could come any day now. When she sees the painting, Esther screams and drops to the ground.

Bacon and I manage to revive his wife and help her back to the wagon. I wonder what caused her to faint. Is it the upsetting picture of the storm, or the face of Bartholomieux? I haven't thought about the man in a while, but on the way back to our wagon, I can't help but wonder about the man who caused so much trouble in town last year.

Saturday, May 4

There is just one more day of marching before we get a break. I don't mind walking along, but it would be nice to have a break. It is a bright, sunny, spring day, and I'm determined to enjoy it now that the wind has finally subsided.

At breakfast, Andrew confirms the weather will remain pleasant, but then he turns his head, grabs his stomach, and doubles over.

"Are you alright, Andrew? Do you need to lie down?"

Andrew stands up straight. "I'm okay, Mama. But something is wrong. I have a bad feeling, and I can't tell why."

When we stop for dinner at midday, Larkin, Stillman, Carter, and Esther's children, Ellen and Robbie, walk down to the river to slake their thirst. We have plenty of water in our barrel, so I make a fast fire and heat beans.

Andrew returns to the wagon after visiting up the line. He runs up to our wagon and looks at me with fear in his eyes. "Where's Pa?"

"He went down to the river. Why, what's wrong?"

Before I finish my sentence, Andrew is gone. He runs toward the river as fast as his feet will carry him.

I shake my head. Usually, Andrew is my most sensible child. I stir the beans, move the pan closer to the flames, and make coffee.

When Larkin and Andrew return from the river, Larkin seems annoyed. "What's gotten into you, boy?"

"I think there is something wrong with that water."

"You scared everyone. What did you do that for?" Larkin turns to me. "Andrew shoved Stillman as he was trying to take a drink and chased little Robbie away from the river, like a mad dog." Then Larkin looks back at Andrew. "What kind of superstitious feeling did you have this time?"

Larkin stomps off in a huff, and Andrew turns to me with tears in his eyes. "They drank the water, Mama."

I place my hand on the boy's back and rub his shoulder. "I'm sure it will be alright, Andrew."

He shakes his head. "No. It won't be alright. Oh, Mama."

With a final pat on his back, I return my attention to the fire. My stomach growls as I scoop beans from the pan. Larkin returns as I stir sugar and lemon extract into water from the barrel, and the other children step toward the fire to grab dinner plates.

After feeding everyone, I gnaw on a biscuit, gaze out over the lonely prairie, and look at my family. I wish I could make them a big meal, with meat, potatoes, vegetables, and pie. I think about Christmas dinner, and Thanksgiving as I watch Larkin and the children devour my beans. They've learned to gobble dinner fast, before the trumpet sounds.

There is barely enough time to stow our provisions and douse the fire before nine blasts signal our next departure. Sometimes, I'm overcome with optimism as we grow closer to our goal, mile by mile. Today, Andrew has me spooked. As the afternoon passes, step by step, a sense of doom that I can't explain grows within me.

In the middle of the afternoon, we reach a small creek. On the other side, I see the lead wagons forming a circle, and my heart skips a beat. A sense of relief washes over me. I'm glad that we'll be stopping early today. Perhaps, that is just what we need to comfort Andrew, and chase away our doubts.

Andrew and Christopher take care of the stock, and Rose leads Ridge back down to the river. Larkin stretches out on the prairie and moans. "I don't want to mention it, but I don't feel so good." He moans and cusses Andrew for bringing sickness upon him, as if it is our son's fault that Larkin doesn't feel good.

"Larkin, Andrew was trying to protect you. It isn't his fault you drank that water. He tried to stop you."

My husband grumbles. "You're right. You're always right. It's not the boy's fault. It's my fault. Everything is my fault. Everything is *always* my fault." He writhes in the grass.

I admonish him. "Stop talking like that, Larkin. How can I help? What do you need?"

Agapito rides up on Rio. "This is Thirtytwo Mile Creek. We will spend Sunday here, and then we will leave the Little Blue River for good. On Monday, we will make our way toward the Platte River, yes?" Agapito looks at me, nods his head toward Larkin, and says, "*¿Qué?* What is wrong with him?"

Larkin answers, telling Agapito how he feels.

Agapito looks at me and says, "Bring him water from your barrel. I'll be back." I run to get the dipper from the side of the wagon as Agapito rides into the next camp.

When Agapito returns, he says that we must separate from the others. He shouts at Andrew and Christopher, "Get the oxen, yes?" When the boys return with the teams, Agapito helps them harness the teams, and then he drives our wagon two hundred yards downstream from the other wagons. Then, Agapito uses our oxen to drag Stillman and Carter's wagon off beside ours, and after that, he does the same with Bacon and Esther's wagon.

He tells us, "Boss Wheel has ordered you to stay away from the other passengers until the sickness has run its course. Healthy people are to stay on this side of the wagons." With an arm, he indicates the north side. "Anyone who is sick must remain to the south of the wagon. I will set up a tent."

Andrew says, "The sickness comes from the water. We can't catch it from each other."

Agapito tilts his head toward the boy. "You may be right, but we can not take any chances. Get me fresh water and rags, yes? Say your prayers. *¡Vamos!*"

Esther paces Agapito's boundary, complaining about being separated from her children. Bacon has given up trying to calm his wife, leaving her to waddle back and forth like a horse looking for an opening along a fence.

I settle the children beside a crackling fire. Rose busies herself with her diary, and Andrew writes a newspaper article while Christopher distracts Dahlia Jane with made-up stories. My heart bleeds for them. They must be so scared.

In the next wagon, Dembi Koofai attaches a large, triangular-shaped flag to a long staff. It looks like something that belongs on a pirate ship. As he carries it toward the isolated wagons, I realize it's meant to be a warning and conveys the danger of contagion.

How can I help those in need? There has to be something I can do. Then it comes to me, I unstrap the water barrel from the side of our wagon, wrap my arms around it, and heft it from its shelf on the side of our wagon. It's a long way to go, and I wonder if I can make it on my own. There's a growing pain in my arms and back as I haul it, very slowly, step by step toward Agapito's infirmary. As I get closer, Agapito sees me and hurries to help me lower the barrel.

"Thank you, Dorcas."

"How are the patients?"

"They do not look so good." He casts me a sympathetic glance. "We must prepare for the worst. We could lose all of them."

My hand covers my face. I can't believe what I'm hearing. "All of them?"

He nods, sadly. "They have cholera, Dorcas."

I feel light-headed, almost dizzy and worry for a moment that I might be infected too. "It can't be, Agapito. It just can't be so."

He tells me he is sorry and that I will need to be strong.

My throat is dry and I swallow hard. Suddenly, I remember purchasing cholera drops from Mr. Ray in Independence. "Wait here. I'll be right back."

When I present the medicinal lozenges, Agapito frowns. "Those might offer some comfort, but they are not a cure. I wish I did not have to tell you that." He takes the cholera drops and turns away.

I bite my lip and tell myself how foolish it is to believe in miracle cures.

Carter bursts from the opening of a tent and darts behind a large blanket Agapito has hung over a couple of posts driven into the prairie dirt.

"They have the skitters, Dorcas. There is a privy behind that blanket." I glance to the side of the blanket at a smaller version of the make-shift latrine. Agapito says, "That is for Ellen."

I ask, "Should I get Dr. Appleyard?"

"No. He can not help us now. When cholera strikes, there is nothing we can do but wish, hope, and pray." He looks at the sky and holds up a hand like he's trying to decide which direction the wind is blowing. "We will know by dark whether there is a chance that anyone survives."

"How do you know?"

"It was the same last year. Also, I had it a few years ago. I was one of the lucky ones. Cholera is bad news. It can strike at any time, and nobody knows where it comes from. We have never heard of anybody getting it twice, so when cholera strikes, I take care of those who get sick."

"Andrew claims that it comes from drinking bad water. Larkin, Stillman, Carter, Ellen, and Robbie went to the river together when we stopped. Doesn't the fact that all of them got sick prove that it comes from bad water?"

"It would seem so."

I amble back toward my family. After I peek around the wagon and see the children beside the campfire, I drop to the ground, bury my face in my hands, and cry. I try to silence my sobs. My body convulses, and I can't stop.

My emotions spiral out of control until I feel a small hand on my back. A child needs me, and I regain my composure in an instant. I turn to see Andrew. He twists his face in knots and looks like he will cry. I hold my arms wide and engulf him in a hug, while kneeling. My knees dig into the dirt.

I start to feel better until I hear Agapito's voice. He clears his throat. I look up from the ground into his eyes, and he shakes his head from side to side. I send Andrew back to the campfire, and Agapito extends his hand to help me climb to my feet. I have trouble standing and my legs wobble as I struggle to keep my body upright.

Urgently, Agapito says, "Get my scouts and tell them to bring shovels. Carter is gone."

I cover my face with both hands. "Oh, that poor child." The image of Stillman and Carter's passionate embrace appears in my mind. I will never forget the shock of seeing that. I tell Agapito, "I'll be right back."

When I return, Agapito looks into my eyes as he tells the scouts that he wants them to start digging graves. “I do not know how many we will need, but it is better to have a hole and not need it than to need one and not have it.”

For a few minutes, I watch as Arikta and Dembi Koofai dig. Agapito carries Carter’s body from the tent and lays it on the ground. I say a prayer, though God doesn’t have much of a history of answering my pleas. Then, I turn toward my wagon, pull a shovel from its peg, and join the scouts.

The curved blade of the shovel punches into the earth, and I heave dirt from the deepening hole until I’m standing waist-deep in the ground. I stop to take a breath and look toward the tents. Agapito emerges carrying another body, and I collapse into the pit, clutching the spade.

Larkin is dead.

Dembi Koofai climbs into the grave I’ve dug, and he helps me stand.

Agapito bends over and sets Larkin’s body on the ground beside Carter. I feel like I am hanging above the prairie, observing the scene from far away. Agapito’s cheeks glisten, and I am touched that my husband’s death has affected him.

What will I tell the children? I think back and try to recall Larkin's last words. The last thing I can remember him saying is, "Everything is *always* my fault." I'd prefer to find a better way to remember him than with those words.

Agapito pries the shovel from my fingers, drops it to the ground, takes me by the hand, and leads me back toward my wagon. “Your children need their mother now, Dorcas. I am sorry.”

I look at Agapito. A question forms on my lips, but I can’t think of words to say. Then I turn away from him.

Where is my black dress? I climb aboard and move boxes until I find one at the bottom of a stack. The dress is wrinkled, but who cares? I haven’t worn this since Armand Bartholomieux's funeral. It was snug the last time I put it on, but today, it fits perfectly.

I kneel on the ground and tell my children that their father is dead. I wrap my arms around my children, and look off toward the west, beyond them. I am done crying. My children need me to be strong. Henceforth, I shall wear the black dress, and mourn without tears. When they have cried themselves dry, I say, "Let's all sleep in the wagon tonight. Get ready for bed. I shall return as soon as I can."

Halfway back to the infirmary, Rose catches up to me. "I want to go with you, Mama."

"I don't know, honey. It is disturbing to look at dead bodies, Rose. Especially the remains of people we love."

She says, "I know, Mama. I want to go. I have to go with you."

I hear Larkin's voice in my head, telling me not to coddle the children. Despite my better judgment, I take Rose's hand and walk toward the freshly-dug graves.

I gasp at the sight of Ellen Prindle. In a few short hours, the child transformed from a healthy-looking ten-year-old to an emaciated corpse, with blueish-black skin, and bulging eyes. Rose kneels beside the little girl and pulls her eyelids closed.

Agapito says, "We must bury them now."

I ask, "Should we get Captain Meadows? I mean, Reverend Meadows."

"No, Boss Wheel will not allow him to come. Not today."

"Should we get Esther?"

Rose says, "No, Mama. Ellen doesn't want Esther to see her like this."

Agapito agrees with Rose. "I do not think that Esther is strong enough, Dorcas."

I look at Agapito. "Have we dug deeply enough? I can't bear to have the wolves rob these graves."

"Yes, Dorcas. It is deep enough. And tomorrow, you can trample the graves with the oxen and wagon wheels, so that the dead can rest in peace."

Rose stands and begins to dance, slowly and gracefully. She drops a shoulder and prances in a circular motion across the prairie. Then, she drops her other shoulder and circles away in the opposite direction. She almost looks like a bird.

After a few minutes, Rose returns, drops to her knees, and gently kisses Larkin's blue lips. She touches his gaunt cheeks with her fingertips, and I'm surprised when she pulls bulky scissors from her pocket. Rose kneels, with her face inches from Larkin's, and painstakingly snips the hair from his head, the whiskers from his cheeks, and his long, wiry mustache, my husband's endless obsession. Why doesn't the child let Larkin take it with him? At first, I step toward her, with the thought of telling her to stop. Instead, Larkin's voice appears in my memory, telling me to leave the children be. Would he want his paternal advice to extend to his burial preparations? It will have to be so. When Rose is finished, Larkin hardly looks recognizable.

Rose walks back to our wagon without a word to anyone. My sense of time evaporates as the minutes go by, and I relive the memory of our time together, as man and wife. We had many happy moments together. I should have never expected Larkin to be somebody he couldn't be, but what difference does that make now? The flickers of our life together shuffle through my mind like a deck of cards. Finally, I remember watching my husband dance with his daughter, days ago, while Bacon and Agapito fiddled, and blink my eyes dry.

I watch the scouts lower the bodies into their graves, Carter to one side, the child in the middle, and Larkin in the hole I dug. Agapito says a few words. When the first shovelful of dirt hits Larkin's body, I feel my body grow tense. They should have coffins instead of being buried as they are.

I've had enough. I turn away and walk toward the tents. Agapito calls out to me. "You must not, Dorcas. It is forbidden. We cannot risk spreading the disease."

Without turning, I reach my arm back behind me and wave off his concern. I crouch in front of the tent and crawl toward Stillman. He has a vacant look in his brown eyes. His skin is pale but not blue, like the corpses outside. He turns his head, looks blankly at me, and says, "Carter is gone."

"I know, honey. I'm so sorry."

"And Larkin, too?"

"Yes, Larkin and Ellen Prindle, also." I glance at Robbie Prindle, who is sleeping peacefully a few feet away.

I place my hands beneath the skinny young man's arms and pull him into a sitting position on my lap. Then, I pull him into my bosom. "We can grieve together, Stillman." I tip his head back and look into his injured face. A tear squeezes from his eye. "Nobody will ever understand what we've been through——nobody but you and me, Stillman. We need each other. Will you fight for me? And for Carter? It's up to you to live life like you are living it for the both of you now."

My lips brush the young man's cheek and I return him to his position on the ground. I cover him with a blanket and pull it up to his chin. With a gentle pat on his chest, and words to let him know I love him, I slither back through the tent flaps.

For a minute, I stand alone on the prairie. Before sinking over the edge of the horizon, the giver of light paints the clouds bright, butterfly-colored orange. There are touches of crimson, pink, and yellow, but mostly, the sky is the color of pumpkins and maple leaves in autumn.

There is an impossible choice to make. Should we continue on to Oregon, or return home after coming so far? Oregon was our dream together. Do I still want to go to Oregon without Larkin?

A wolf howls. The hair on the back of my neck stands on end. A pair of carnivorous eyes watch me from the river's edge, and I slowly back away toward the wagon's protection.

After a devastating tragedy, Dorcas Moon faces brutal choices in the unforgiving wilderness. An unsolved hometown murder casts a foreboding shadow over their journey. Mounting responsibilities weigh heavy on her shoulders. Start reading *Lighten the Load at https://books2read.com/Lighten-the-Load* to continue the adventure of a lifetime as Dorcas confronts the challenges that shape her destiny.

I hope to become one of your favorite new authors. Sign up for my email list at https://www.itsoag.com/contact so you can stay up-to-date on upcoming releases, special offers, and exclusive giveaways. As a thank you, I'll send you a special, Ghosts Along the Oregon Trail word search puzzle.

Jump Back In

Don't let the dust settle on your wagon!

Scan the QR code and leap to David Fitz-Gerald's website where you can find the links to the next installment in Ghosts Along the Oregon Trail.

About the Author

David Fitz-Gerald writes westerns and historical fiction. He is the author of twelve books, including the brand-new series, Ghosts Along the Oregon Trail set in 1850. He's a multiple Laramie Award, first place, best in category winner; a Blue Ribbon Chanticleerian; a member of Western Writers of America; and a member of the Historical Novel Society.

Alpine landscapes and flashy horses always catch Dave's eye and turn his head. He is also an Adirondack 46-er, which means that he has hiked to the summit of the range's highest peaks. As a mountaineer, he's happiest at an elevation of over four thousand feet above sea level.

Dave is a lifelong fan of western fiction, movies, and music. It should be no surprise that Dave delights in placing memorable characters on treacherous trails, mountain tops, and on the backs of wild horses.

Don't miss Book 2 in the Ghosts Along the Oregon Trail series. Jump aboard for *Lighten the Load*.

David Fitz-Gerald
www.itsoag.com

A Tip of the Hat

This series is affectionately dedicated to the countless authors whose words have preserved the legend of the Oregon Trail, the diligent historians who have meticulously chronicled its history, and the brave emigrants who embarked on a perilous journey in pursuit of lofty dreams. Additionally, this series pays tribute to the indigenous peoples whose ancestors lived, loved, and died in these lands since ancient times. The rugged peaks and fruited plains, simultaneously abundant and inhospitable, bore witness to their stories. May their tales always echo through the canyons of history, preserving the spirit and honoring the legacy of those who walked the path before planes, trains, and automobiles.

Thank you to the collaborators that helped me bring Ghosts Along the Oregon Trail to life: editors Kolton Fitz-Gerald and Lindsay Fitzgerald; singer songwriter Kyle Hughes; White Rabbit Arts at the Historical Fiction Company; and the coaches at Author Ad School.

Deep gratitude to my Facebook readers' group, Adirondack Spirit Guides. I appreciate the guidance, support, and early reader feedback. A special nod to Gail Cook, who was the first to make it through the series. Thank you: Cha Abangan, Danielle Apple, Susan Barker, Deva Beeks, Elizabeth Bell, Paul Bennett, Cecil Betit, Kathleen Bianchi, Bill Buwalda,

Wendy Cadieux, Janette Carraway Reynolds, Kate Clifford Eminhizer, Meg Collins, Gail Cook, Tracy Dahl Urschler, Darlene Deans, Keegan Farr, Jeffrey Fitz-Gerald, Patti Fitz-Gerald, D.A. Galloway, Linda Garnett, Janette Gillot, Pam Hough Rogers, Shelbie Howard, Lisa Hunt, TJ London, Jacqueline Marie, Dee Marley, Sandy Miller, Maggie Muir, Steve Murray, Sheila Myers, Anita Ogden, Mary Jane O'Neill, Cody Marie Phoenix, Seth Rain, Dave Reed, Conchita Selvo, Lori Lee Sills, Debra Smith, Chelsie Stanford, Mattie Terrell, Pat Wahler, Quinta Wilkinson, Michelle Willms, and Cindy Yarber Turner.

This project also pays homage to a genre that I've loved as long as I can remember. The old west in fiction, history books, landscape paintings, movies, television and songs inspired this project. If you think a character name is similar to an iconic western hero, you're not mistaken. Some of the characters' names were pulled from the roots of my family tree. For example, a woman named Dorcas is my 6th great-grandaunt. Many monikers are plucked from film credits. The unusual character, Fritz Franzwa is named to honor the work of a dedicated historian who researched, documented, and published *The Oregon Trail Revisited* and *Maps of the Oregon Trail*, which helped me cast my fictional emigrants on credible trail.

During my research for this project, I had the opportunity to visit many of the Oregon Trail's landmarks. It could take a lifetime to visit them all, but I'm well on my way. I've had the pleasure of crisscrossing the historic trail on the scenic byways in Wyoming and Nebraska, and I recall a sweltering day during a record-breaking heatwave in the 1980s. My brother, Jeff, and I visited the mostly abandoned town of Jeffrey City, Wyoming, which boasted a population of three. It's situated near the Oregon Trail and the Sweetwater River. We purchased soft drinks, but by the time we made it back to the truck, the red cans had already gone warm. It was *that* hot. The truck wasn't air conditioned, and I remember sympathizing with the pioneers, trudging along beside a chain of wagons. More recently, I had the pleasure of visiting the National Frontier Trails Museum in Independence, Missouri; the Fort Bridger State Historic Site; and the White Mountain Petroglyphs. It's off the trail, but I just had to send my characters there.

I'm *most* grateful to *you* for stepping away from the present, into the distant past with me. Thank you. I'd love to hear from you. If you get a chance to drop me an email at dave@itsoag.com, I'd love to know: if you were alive in 1850, would you have chosen to follow the Oregon Trail?

Appendix 1 – Wagons and Cast

Characters in bold are real. Otherwise, they're fictional.

Wagon #1 (Fort Wayne, Indiana)

Captain Mortimer Meadows, 38

Luella Meadows, 35

Cassie Meadows, 17

Gideon Meadows, 15

Wagon #2 (Fort Wayne, Indiana)

Wade Crouse, 35

Dottie Crouse, 34

Wagon #3 (Fort Wayne, Indiana)

Travis Latham, 32

Catherine Latham, 26

Lucy Latham, 7

Lemuel Latham, 5

Wagon #4 (Falls Village, Connecticut)
Artemus Weaver, 22
Grace Young Weaver, 21

Wagon #5 (Portsmouth, New Hampshire)
Lloyd Carpenter, 27
Hetty Shaw Carpenter, 25
Elizabeth Carpenter, 6
Annie Carpenter, 4
Sally Carpenter, 3

Wagon #6 (Portsmouth, New Hampshire)
Minor Shaw, 70
Ellenanne Shaw, 52

Wagon #7 (St. Louis, Missouri)
Leon Humphries, 24

Wagon #8 (Newark, New Jersey)
Clarkson Sawyer, 23
Bridget Pierce Sawyer, 22
Theodore (Teddy) Sawyer, 3

Wagon #9 (Newark, New Jersey)
Sullivan (Sully) Pierce, 60

Wagon #10 (Evanston, Indiana)
Schuyler Steele, 21

Wagon #11 (Frankfurt, Germany)
Wilhelm Lett, 39
Frida Lett 38
Berta Lett, 19
Katrin Lett, 17
Bianka Lett, 16
Carl Lett, 15

Wagon #12 (Madison, Georgia)
Horace Blocker, 36
Lana Blocker, 29
Adam Blocker, 8

Wagon #13 (Skibbereen, West Cork, Ireland)
Cian Reid, 20
Oona Reid, 19
Aengus Reid, infant

Wagon #14 (Richmond, Virginia)
Dr. Hollis Appleyard, 45
Charlotte Appleyard, 42
Martin Appleyard, 19
Violet Appleyard, 17

Wagon #15
Wagon Master Joseph (Boss Wheel) Roulette, 40
Assistant Wagon Master Agapito (Pito) Huerta Delgado, 31
Pawnee Scout Arikta (Eagle), 19
Shoshone Scout Dembi Koofai (Stone Face), 20

Wagon #16 (Wilmington, New York)
Larkin Moon, 35
Dorcas Moon, 34
Rose Marie Moon, 12
Andrew Moon, 11
Christopher Moon, 9
Dahlia Jane Moon, 4

Wagon #17 (Champlain, New York)
Stillman Southmaid, 18
Carter Wilson, 20

Wagon #18 (Lake Placid, New York)
Charlie Oliver (Cobb) Banyon, 29
Jennie Banyon, 25
Bess Banyon, 6
Joe Banyon, 4

Wagon #19 (Wilmington, New York)
Bacon Bump, 46
Esther Prindle Bump, 41
Robbie Prindle, 13
Ellen Prindle, 10

Wagon #20 (Wilmington, New York)
Pious Bull, 37
Addie Bull, 36
Pious Bull (PBJ) Jr, 18

Mary Bull, 17

Leander Bull, 11

Wagon #21 (Driftwood, Pennsylvania)

Robert (Bobby) Bond, 20

Serena Horton Bond, 19

Wagon #22 (Driftwood, Pennsylvania)

Wayne Horton, 21

Drucilla Bond Horton, 18

Wagon #23 (Portage, Pennsylvania)

Galusha Gains, 28

Pamela Gains, 27

Henry Gains, 9

Margaret Gains, 7

Wagon #24 (Portage, Pennsylvania)

Samuel Grosvenor, 24

Edna Grosvenor, 20

Sarah Grosvenor, 2

Wagon #25 (Springfield, Illinois)

Roy Franklin, 22

Peg Franklin, 21

Wagon #26 (Hillsborough, North Carolina)

Garland Knox, 14

Hannah Knox, 55

Miranda Knox, 52

Wagon #27 (Charleston, South Carolina)

Butler Grimes, 26

Betty Grimes, 25

Dean Grimes, 6

Lulu Grimes, 4

Wagon #28 (Falls Village, Connecticut)

Landon Young, 24

Cornelia Young, 20

Landon Young Jr, 3

Wagon #29 (Washington, DC)

Fritz Franzwa, 40

Minna Franzwa, 19

Alma Franzwa, 18

Bruno Franzwa, 17

Oskar Franzwa, 15

Lilly Franzwa, 7

Wagon #30 (Columbus, Ohio)

Foster Bellows, 27

Indiana Bellows, 24

Horace Bellows, 5

Wagon #31 (Cumberland, Maryland)

Alvah Nye, 20

Outlaws:

Lennox (The Viper) McAdams, 24

Leon McAdams, 22

Sloan McAdams, 21

Ross (The Radish) McAdams, 18

Ghosts:

Armand Bartholomieux;

Katherine, The Lady in Green

Olivia McAdams

Sacagawea

Clayton Stonecipher

Oregon City:

Sarah Young Terwilliger

Brulé:

Spotted Tail

Snarling Wolf (Song Manitu Tanka Glow)

Fort Bridger:

Alvah “Lucky” Nye (the elder)

Ol’ Gabe (Jim Bridger)

Ol’ Vaskiss (Luis Vasquez)

Peddler, George "Muddy George" Traverse

Shoshone:

Chief Washakie

Crimson Dawn

Sees Through Clouds

Independence, Missouri:
Attorney, Mr. Biles
Shopkeeper, Mr. Ray

On the trail:
Larry Pritchard
Miner, Henry Trudgeon

Fort Hall:
Abigail "Gail" Trudgeon
Tinker, Burton Potts

Fort Boise:
Shopkeeper, Jeremy "Remy" Bascombe

Meek Cutoff:
Linc Collie

Barlow Gate:
Chet Westerly

Philip Foster Farm:
Philip Foster

Appendix 2—Animals

Oxen

Hardtack, a Devon (Moon family)

Scrapple, a Devon (Moon family)

Horses

Blizzard, a black and white, whorled, Andalusian (Dorcas Moon)

Rio, a golden buckskin with a black mane and socks (Agapito Huerta Delgado)

Howl, a piebald (black and white) paint (Arikta)

Coffeepot, a black appaloosa (Dembi Koofai)

Gwibunzi, a skewbald (brown and white) paint, mustang with a black tail and black, brown, and white mane (Dorcas Moon)

Clipper, a black horse (Boss Wheel)

Roni, a red roan horse (Dorcas Moon)

Monsoon, a big bay (bright reddish brown with black mane and socks) (Alvah Nye)

Flossie, aka Motherlode, a gold sniffing mule (Miner Henry Trudgeon)

Donkey (Peddler, Muddy George Traverse)

Dogs

Honey, a three-year-old black Labrador retriever (Alvah Nye)

Chestnut, a five-year-old Irish Setter (Landon and Cordelia Young)

Other Animals

Ridge, a devil-eyed goat (Moon Family)

Gloria, a broody hen (Moon Family)

Made in the USA
Las Vegas, NV
30 December 2024